DIXIE BROWNING
A Secret Valentine

Silhouette *Romance*

Published by Silhouette Books New York

America's Publisher of Contemporary Romance

SILHOUETTE BOOKS, a Simon & Schuster Division of
GULF & WESTERN CORPORATION
1230 Avenue of the Americas, New York, N.Y. 10020

ISBN: 0-671-57203-2

First Silhouette Books printing February, 1983

10 9 8 7 6 5 4 3 2 1

Map by Ray Lundgren

"No More Games, Grace.

A man can only stand so much and stay sane."

One large arm pinned her in place. When she tried to duck under his elbow he blocked her with his body, pressing her heavily against the door.

She writhed beneath him to escape this prison of passion, but he only laughed, a gleam of satisfaction—or was it triumph—in his eyes.

"Quinn, behave yourself!" She adopted her best schoolmarm tone and heard it come out as a breathless whisper.

"Not now, Grace—behaving myself is the furthest thing from my mind."

In spite of herself she trembled with needing him . . . just before she felt the touch of his lips.

DIXIE BROWNING
is a native of North Carolina. Many of her stories are born as she travels from her home in Winston-Salem to her cottage in Frisco on Hatteras Island. She is also an accomplished watercolor artist, as well as writer.

Dear Reader:

I'd like to take this opportunity to thank you for all your support and encouragement of Silhouette Romances.

Many of you write in regularly, telling us what you like best about Silhouette, which authors are your favorites. This is a tremendous help to us as we strive to publish the best contemporary romances possible.

All the romances from Silhouette Books are for you, so enjoy this book and the many stories to come. I hope you'll continue to share your thoughts with us, and invite you to write to us at the address below:

Karen Solem
Editor-in-Chief
Silhouette Books
P.O. Box 769
New York, N.Y. 10019

For my one and only Valentine, Lee

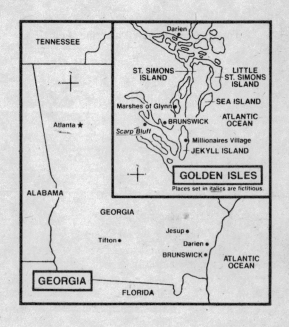

GOLDEN ISLES

Places set in *italics* are fictitious.

Chapter One

The trucks—cobalt blue and clearly marked with the QD emblem of the engineering firm, were already there, and Grace's lips tightened as she saw Terri perched provocatively on the wall, flirting with the construction workers. I could tell you a few things about the dangers of what you're doing, she thought, her slender feet in the tan calf pumps striding briskly along the cracked concrete walk.

Another girl joined Terri and her eager male audience just as Grace reached the door. A sigh of resignation left her lips. When she had first landed this teaching job, she had somehow envisioned herself chatting with her students about their interests—perhaps offering them friendly advice as a sort of older sister.

Unfortunately it hadn't worked out that way. Most of her students were older and far too busy to linger for a cozy talk with teacher, and her one younger group was completely dominated by a handful of boy-crazy troublemakers. And because she had been nervous that first day, she had stiffened up, overreacting to what was probably only a normal testing of any new teacher, and consequently gotten off to an impossible start.

Veering around a group of chattering girls, she wondered, not for the first time, if it had been a mistake to go for a teaching position instead of an office job. Being shut up in an office all day held little appeal, but then, Grace didn't relish being shut up anywhere when she could be outside. Still, in an office she wouldn't have been called on to deal with discipline problems.

You try teaching business arts to a roomful of giddy girls whose minds are on one thing and one thing only! she argued with herself silently. Behind her, a susurrus rose and fell excitedly as a knot of her girls compared wishful notes on their favorite subject.

"Oh, wow, I saw him last night on the way to the mall. He was driving that *incredible* car and the light changed and I felt like throwing myself under the wheels!" one of the girls—it sounded like Carly—vowed.

"I'd rather throw myself under *him!*" another one chimed in feelingly.

"You and me both!"

Grace took a deep breath and adjusted the imaginary ramrod along her spine. She had reached the door of her classroom and now she turned, giving the girls a look of wary friendliness. "Good morning, girls."

"Good morning, Miss Spencer," came the obedient response—so why did it always sound like "Miss Spinster" to her ears?

Applying herself to the task of instructing an assortment of twenty-seven girls fresh out of high school in the intricacies of word processing, Grace closed her mind to the competing attraction just outside the window.

Competing! As if she stood a chance of diverting their attention from the sight of all those brawny, blue-jeaned construction workers swarming all over the grounds! The one who seemed to be some sort of foreman, the one they called the Incredible Hunk, was climbing up on top of that monstrous bulldozer, and even from here it was obvious that one of his men had transgressed. Turning abruptly away from the window, Grace was glad she couldn't hear what he was saying. The air would be turning blue any minute now, if she was any judge!

"Carly, watch for the prompt," Grace repeated with frayed patience. "It will tell you what you've done wrong, and all you have to do is look in your work manual and find out how to correct it."

"Oh, h---!" The girl barely stifled a four-letter word, and Grace fought back the rising tension that was becoming a familiar classroom companion. "Look, why do I have to learn all this junk when I'm planning on being an engineer?"

"Office skills will always be valuable," Grace reminded the red-faced eighteen-year-old. "Last month you were planning to be a paralegal."

"That was *before,*" Carly replied, and Grace didn't have to ask before what? Before that uncouth giant came along to litter the landscape with his monstrous machines and his tightly jeaned, bearded, hard-hatted crew!

At three fifteen she saw her last class file out, checked the room and its equipment hurriedly and snatched up her briefcase. It was Friday, thank the Lord, and for two whole days and three glorious nights she intended to forget she had ever heard of any piece of office equipment more sophisticated than a pencil!

Well . . . not so glorious, at that. She had promised Elliot she would go to dinner and a movie with him. It would be their eleventh date. She could predict the restaurant, the menu and the movie, and she couldn't drum up much excitement over any of it. More's the pity, she admitted to herself as she swung along toward the charming, if somewhat shabby, house where she lived with an assortment of inherited cats and houseplants. Still, she wasn't quite ready at nearly thirty-one to relegate her social life to women's service clubs and Tupperware parties.

The low angle of the autumn sun was kind to her lime-green house. It turned the rust on the galvanized roof to glowing crimson and cast lacy shadows through the moss-hung branches of the liveoak tree. She really should trim back the hanging baskets on the front porch, but they did look lovely, and the window boxes would have made her great-aunt proud.

Allowing her ankles to be massaged by the assortment of cats that met her, she paused to scratch beneath the chin of a battered old giant of a tomcat who draped himself over the porch railing, looking on disdainfully as his harem fawned over her. "I admire your spirit, you old reprobate," Grace purred at him. "Don't give an inch!"

She had checked the mailbox automatically, not allowing herself to admit disappointment when there was no letter from All Seasons Greetings. If Mr. Harris had any good news from the contest, he would have called. If he bothered to write at all, it would be to tell her that they had not won and to encourage her to continue the good work.

Stripping out the pins that held her hair in a tightly confined knot, she looked forward to two days of scribbling and drawing for All Seasons before she had to brace herself for another five days of molding and shaping—hammering and sawing would be more like it—the future secretaries of the world. Or at least of east Georgia.

She stepped out of the tan pumps, wriggling her toes on the patchwork rug she had fashioned from carpet mill samples, and slipped off her stockings. Her dress went next, and she hung it carefully on a hanger before padding out to the kitchen to collect a snack.

The kitchen was impossible, the bathroom even more so, and she determined to brave the powers that be and let her rental agent know that if he didn't do something about the problem, she'd take matters into her own hands.

And he'd say, "Very well, Miss Spencer, we'll see to it that your bathroom and kitchen don't flood every time it rains. Oh, and by the way, your rent will be doubled as of the first of the month."

Oh, he had her over a barrel, all right. Even poor old Uncle Henry had known better than to complain. He had patiently baled out the back part of the house every time it rained rather than risk having his rent raised. It wasn't the roof—that would have been too simple. She could have put pans under a roof leak, but since the house had slowly settled into the earth to the point that it was slightly below ground level in the rear, she was helpless to do anything about it. "Maybe I ought to start drooling over the Incredible Hunk and his pet bulldozer," she muttered to a piece of cheddar. She had done about all she could with her own shovel and seen her feeble efforts washed out time and time again.

Returning to the living room—the back parlor, Uncle Henry had called it—she stretched out on the sofa and elevated her feet. If she was vain about anything at all, it was her feet. They were slender and fine-boned, as were her ankles—as she was herself, only she spent little time thinking about her own looks. Neatness, not beauty, had been the rule at home, but in spite of all her best efforts Grace had never managed to look sharp enough to please her father, Colonel Bergen Spencer, USMC retired. In fact, she could think of no area in which she had managed to please the stern perfectionist—and too many in which she had brought down his harsh judgment on her vulnerable head. Occasionally she wondered if her life might have taken a totally different direction had it not been for the strong and diverse personalities of her immediate family.

Introspection was not her forte—it had been a decidedly uncomfortable exercise for too long now. Still, it was impossible not to wonder how much of her father she had inherited when she found herself reacting to her students' noisy, disorderly behavior by freezing up and barking out ultimatums—which only made matters worse!

Pity she hadn't more of her mother in her—she could have disregarded the whole problem by involving herself in some worthy cause and ignoring the problems existence.

After finishing the sharp cheese and polishing off an apple, she padded into her bedroom to put on a pair of velvety soft jeans and a yellow ribbed knit shirt. The bedroom still smelled faintly of lavender, after all this time. Grace smiled and dragged a brush through her long, finely textured leaf-brown hair, not bothering to glance at a mirror as she braided it into one thick plait that fell slightly off center down her back.

The house had belonged to her great-aunt and -uncle, or at least they had rented it for so long that they considered it theirs. Grace had first seen it when she had been delegated to attend the funeral of her great-aunt Aldonia. The fact that she even had a great-aunt and -uncle had come as a total surprise to her that day when her mother had frowned over the telegram and said, "Hmmm . . . well, I guess one of us ought to go and I certainly can't. There's the bazaar coming up in three weeks, and I've volunteered to organize a benefit for the Children's Home."

Nor could her father. He was far too involved in bringing Hansonville's Civil Defense organization up to his rare standards of perfection. Both her brothers were married, and Bart was expecting his firstborn momentarily, and of course, Jill was still in school.

Feeling slightly guilty, Grace had readily accepted the mission, looking on it as a vacation of sorts. She had been working too hard for too long, as well as going to night school for the past three years, and even though her relationship with her family was normal again on the surface, there was still a certain amount of tension. Things could never be as they had been before—not that they had ever been all that great. Even at the best of times the relationship had always lacked a certain something.

Not discipline. Heaven knows, there had always been plenty of that to go around, although the colonel had mellowed slightly over the years, and Jilly, seven years younger than Grace and a golden-haired, blue-eyed doll from the day she was born, had never come in for her share of his scathing disposition. Both Bart, who was two years older than Grace, and Evan, who was a year younger, had rebelled in turn against the unceasing military-like discipline with which Colonel Spencer ran his home and his family, but they had eventually returned to the fold. Neither of them had followed their father into the Marine Corps, to his eternal sorrow, but as both had finished law school and

Bart was beginning to get involved in politics, the colonel was grudgingly proud of them both.

Grace's rebellion had been another thing altogether. Her father had more or less drummed her out of the family, and her mother, who seldom went against the colonel's commands, had been little help. Bart had been censorious at the time, but what had hurt even more was that he had been unforgivably smug when it had all blown up—leaving Grace's ego, her reputation and her credit rating shot to pieces.

Evan and Jilly had rallied around, and Evan, though himself newly married and paying for a four-bedroom condominium, had helped her through the financial nightmare until she could get on her feet again.

She had paid him back. Jill, bless her, could offer little but love and uncritical support, but that had been an unbelievably welcome commodity.

Living in the same small New England town, although in her own cheap apartment, Grace had gradually reinstated herself with her family. It had not been easy. At times she had wondered if it was even worth the effort, but they were her family, and probably the only one she would ever have, and she had kept at it until she was once more able to join them for the occasional Sunday dinner and family birthday parties.

By the time the telegram from Brunswick, Georgia, had come, she was near exhaustion from years of work and night school, but she had found herself immediately warming to Uncle Henry. He had been ailing even then, having just barely recovered from the flu that had taken his wife of the past fifty-three years. Grace had put off going home again and again until it was too late. Not only did she love the slower pace of the small southern town, she had also come to love her droll, gentle relative. The fact that his health was slowly declining had made her decision easier, and Grace told herself there was no way she could have left him to potter around the old house alone, not eating enough, not taking his blood pressure medicine. There were no close neighbors on the winding, unpaved road by the edge of the picturesque marsh, and besides, she felt more relaxed in the shabby old house with Uncle Henry than she had in years—than she *ever* had at home.

The town, the house and the lifestyle had suited her from the beginning, and she and Henry had suited each other. They had fallen into a pleasant rut that had lasted until Henry had died, eleven months after his wife. Grace had been working as a temporary receptionist in a doctor's office, and the decision to stay on had been made with no conscious thought. She applied for a teaching position at a local junior college when she had found out that in spite of its name, it was a vocational school that taught business courses on both the adult and high school levels. Now, after her first two months of teaching, she felt reasonably certain that she had settled into a pattern that would grow more comfortable as the years went by, like a pair of new shoes that had to have the stiffness worn away before they really fit.

Her daily bread was assured—at least it would be if she could once get her younger girls under control—and the butter would be provided by All Seasons Greeting Cards Inc., as it had been for the past six years.

If anything good could be said to have come from the disastrous affair with Don, it was that. Someone had mentioned that she ought to try sending her ideas to a greeting card company after seeing the cleverly illustrated rhyming notices she had placed around The Apple Barrel. All Seasons had been closest and she had tried it, astounded when Mr. Harris had liked her things enough to use her as a continuing contributor on a free-lance basis. When she had moved south, she had simply mailed her things in, usually half a dozen or so at a time. Some were accepted, some rejected with scrawled apologies or suggestions for improvement. The pay wasn't great, but the satisfaction kept her soul intact through the bad times.

The temperature was in the sixties, warm for someone from Vermont, but her blood had thinned since she had moved south. After grabbing a sweater, Grace let herself out and headed for her favorite place of inspiration—*one* of her favorites, she amended silently. If the romantic marshes, the sprawling liveoaks and sturdy little palmettos in her own neighborhood weren't enough, there were the nearby Sea Islands. Within walking or easy driving distance she had all the material she'd ever need. Her drawings, whimsical though botanically quite accurate, had been used on a line of regional stationery as well as the greeting cards that were All Seasons' main line. The hardest task was to relate the drawings to her jingles, which tended to be blatantly sentimental, but she was gradually building a following for her offbeat work, according to Mr. Harris. She'd probably never be able to support herself on her earnings as a writer of bad verse and an artist of small talent, but now and then the firm entered one of her designs in the annual industry-wide competition, promising to split the rewards when and if it won.

Last year she had come in third with a child's birthday card, and Mr. Harris had sent her the small pewter loving cup bearing the inscription "All Seasons Greeting Cards, Inc., 1982, Third Place."

Leaving her briefcase at home, she tucked her smaller portfolio and India ink pen under her arm as she dodged the dried mud in the low spots along the road. Three days without rain and the dust rose behind each footstep. Throwing back her head in an unconscious attitude of pleasure, she lengthened her stride and breathed in the mingled odors of the salt marshes, the pulp and paper factory and the pleasant, creosotey smell from the nearby naval stores manufacturer.

The scrubby growth that bordered Sidney Lanier's beloved Marshes of Glynn was all but impenetrable in places as Grace followed the narrow, winding road to a small clearing she had come to think of as her sanctuary. There wasn't a house in sight, although the traffic from Glynn Avenue came faintly through the sighing of the pines. It was her own private place, a place where she could forget the tensions that grew out of wrestling with a subject she knew she was temperamentally unsuited to teach—heavens, she didn't even like digital watches! But for Don, she'd probably be starving in an art colony somewhere.

Forget Don! Forget the past and try not to think about that curiously empty feeling that came over her at unexpected times lately. So she was past thirty and her life was devoid of any deep personal commitment. So what? If the past had taught her anything, it was that there's little to be gained from personal relationships except pain and humiliation. She had everything in her well-ordered life any sensible woman could want, and if she wanted male companionship, there was always Elliot.

The seat of her pants was growing damp and her feet were cold. The late November warmth had gone with the setting sun, and now the sky was washed in a pale alizarin light that dyed the acres of marsh a blushing pink. Idly Grace picked up a chunk of marl, a remnant of some long-past attempt at improving the unused road, and stroked its ancient shell-shape. New developments were encroaching on both sides, with paved streets and all the usual city-type facilities, but her own few acres had been left untouched, thank goodness.

She had not gone more than a hundred feet along the road when she heard the sound of an approaching vehicle. Except for the meter reader and an occasional stray tourist, there had never been any traffic here. The very loneliness of the place was one of its chief attractions.

Grace waited until the vehicle was close behind her before stepping off into a clump of saw palmettos. She wondered what business anyone had on a road that led from nowhere to nowhere, but she was determined not to allow the intrusion to spoil her tranquil mood. She didn't even know who owned the tract of land on which Uncle Henry's house, the last survivor of a bygone age, sagged slowly into old age. During the time she had lived here, she had enjoyed almost complete privacy— so much so that she had come to think of the place as her own.

Now the tranquil atmosphere was shattered by the sight of a familiar cobalt-blue pickup. Suddenly all the daily frustrations of competing with QD's construction workers for her students' attention boiled up in her again, and at the tough, gutsy roar her hard-won sangfroid deserted her. The truck came around the curve too fast and, thoroughly exasperated, Grace hurled the stone to the ground. It bounced away, lost in the cloud of dust thrown up by the retreating truck.

Only the vehicle was no longer retreating. Before the cloud of dust even began to settle, the engine noise ceased and the sound of a rock striking metal rang out like a shot in the hushed atmosphere.

Oh, blast! How was she to know the rock would

ricochet? It was precisely the childish sort of behavior that had gotten her in trouble with her father years ago. She smiled reluctantly—if her students could see her now!

She couldn't even accuse the truck of trespassing. After all, she didn't own the road, and the driver couldn't help it if it happened to be a particularly dusty one. And that was always true unless the road was under water, which happened whenever the marsh tides were higher than normal or after a heavy rain.

Even as she stepped back onto the road and walked slowly toward the stationary pickup truck, she began rationalizing her reaction. QD Engineering had made discipline in her classroom a farce for the past two months. It had reached the point where two of the girls were in danger of failing simply because they couldn't keep their eyes on a terminal when the prevailing view was one of a dozen or so young men with shirts open down to their low-riding belts. Grace was temperamentally unsuited to be a disciplinarian at the best of times—a result of having a martinet of a father, no doubt—but thanks to a macho crew of heavy construction workers, she had yet even to *see* the best of times!

As she neared the truck she slowed unconsciously, cutting a wary glance toward the high, blue cab. The driver was barely visible through a window made all but opaque by a low-angled sun and a thick coat of dust, but there was no mistaking the arrogant angle of that head, the breadth of those shoulders. It was the one they called the Incredible Hunk. Even without a guilty conscience Grace found the man intimidating. He was scaled to the enormous machines he operated, although from the few times she had seen him at relatively close range, she knew there wasn't an ounce of superfluous fat on his monumental frame. She had gone no more than a few feet past the truck when she heard the opening and slamming of the door.

"Girl!"

Girl? Grace refused to dignify the impertinent summons with recognition. Her stiff-legged stride was as long as she could manage, given her modest height.

"Wait!" the man called out after her. She veered off onto an almost invisible animal track—she didn't have to hang around and apologize just because she had accidentally struck his pickup. Was that the sound of footfalls crackling through the dried weeds? She quickened her steps. Then, just as her imagination was beginning to get out of hand, she heard the truck door slam. The engine snarled and caught.

He was leaving! Chiding herself for overreacting, she expelled her breath in a relieved gust, and then her eyes narrowed. *Was* he leaving? The powerful engine was barely ticking over as if he'd had second thoughts about going.

Her brain must have atrophied! She had fallen so easily into the comfortable pattern of life here in Brunswick, settling into an easygoing friendliness with the people at school, the mailman, the women at her favorite seafood market. Her innate shyness, the lack of self-confidence she had fought against all her life, had gradually given way to a wary relaxation, and then to an open enjoyment of the genuine warmth of the people she came into contact with.

And now she was going to pay for it! Facing a roomfull of arrogant, unruly teenage girls was nothing compared to facing a muscle-bound construction worker whose truck she had managed to scratch!

She was still standing there when the engine was cut again, and a large figure swung down from the cab and moved the few yards into the underbrush to confront her. Bracing herself, she lifted her chin, determined not to plead. "Please—please, you don't understand—it was an accident. I didn't mean it."

"You didn't mean what?"

The thunder of her heart almost choked her as she tried to moisten dry lips with an even dryer tongue. "I—I didn't mean to hit your truck."

The man stepped over a clump of prickly pear, and she edged back a foot. He wore an orange hard hat with a blue QD on the front, and his body, in creased khakis and immense, dusty boots, was as big as a fortress. He came a few steps nearer, half silhouetted against the fading light, and Grace backed away, extending a defensive hand in front of her. He halted, removing the hat to reveal a face she had only seen at a distance, on top of the big yellow machine that had cleared the ground for the new dormitory. The eyebrows alone—thick, black as tar and arched over obsidian eyes, would have set it apart, even without the mustache. That was thick, well trimmed and salted with gray.

When he spoke, his voice was a curiously gentle rumble. "Did you hit my truck?"

Was he playing with her? Of course she had hit his truck! She might have broken a window, for all she knew! She'd been afraid to look closely as she stalked past it. "Look, I apologize. It was an accident. If I scratched your paint, I'll pay for it, but please, leave me alone. I—I'd pay for it now, but I don't have any money with me—see? Just a portfolio. Papers, that's all." This was not the sort of man one angered. In spite of his rumpled, workmanlike clothes he carried himself with an air of authority that didn't come from wrestling with heavy equipment—not if she was any judge of men. He sent out waves of *something* that registered on every raw nerve in her body, and whatever it was, it had the effect of jamming her mental processes. She was staring at him like an idiot, unable to come up with a single coherent thought, much less a diversionary tactic.

"Look, honey, stop quaking in your boots. I don't want your money and I'm not turned on by little girls with pigtails, although I'd offer a word of advice—don't wander around all by yourself on deserted roads this time of day. The least that could happen to you is that you could be sideswiped. It's hard as the devil to see against the sun when your windshield's plastered over with dust."

Some of the painful rigidity drained from her backbone. "You mean I didn't hurt your truck?"

"No, baby doll, you didn't hurt my truck." He grinned, and Grace was illogically struck by the contrast between the white teeth and the dark mustache. She could almost see why the girls were so enthralled by this creature. He wasn't precisely handsome, not in the conventional sense, but there was something about him—something larger than life.

"Then why did you come after me?"

Hooking big, well-shaped thumbs into his wide leather belt, he allowed his grin to fade. "To apologize for the dust bath, for one thing, and to warn you that you're near invisible at this time of day on a dusty road. I'd have slowed down if I'd seen you."

Grace mumbled something about not having expected any traffic and managed to tear her eyes away from the man's face. So this was what the girls were panting after! He had to speak twice before she heard him offer her a ride home.

"No—ah, no thanks."

He swung away then with a casual salute, and Grace watched him drive off with relief. She was long past the hero-worshiping stage her girls were going through, but all the same—the man was so . . . so *vital!* It was a little like standing beside a caged lion. Whether or not one cared for the species, one couldn't help but be impressed. For the sake of her girls' education, she hoped all the carpenters and brick masons that were due to arrive after the initial construction would be fat, bald and misogynous.

Chapter Two

It rained the first three days of the following week, precluding any outside work by the QD crew. To Grace's immense satisfaction several of her morning students showed signs of becoming interested in learning more about the sophisticated business machines today's secretaries would be called on to master. Playing computer games was one thing. Setting up and attaching glossaries and formatting financial reports was something else again.

They applied themselves with surprising diligence, with only a few longing glances at the unpopulated construction site. To her disgust Grace found her own eyes straying more than once to the huge yellow bulldozer parked to one side of the site. The man who had dusted her down the week before was no ordinary bulldozer operator, whatever else he was—she'd be willing to bet on that.

On Thursday the sun shone on a glistening lake of muddy water, and the blue and orange trucks arrived just before eleven.

A day and a half to go before the reprieve. Get through the afternoon plus one more day and you can forget about these infernal contraptions for a whole weekend! The sentiment was echoed by the other teachers, on general principles, but Grace knew that the steady, week-long increase of her own tension was due more to her incompatibility with the subject she taught than to either the students or the schedule. MacCready Vocational Junior College—MCV to its intimates—catered to those women who would be joining the work force rather than going on to the university. With a few notable exceptions they were a more serious group than would be found in the average junior college. Even so, her free time, when she could apply herself to her avocation, was the carrot that kept her going during the work week.

At times she had to remind herself forcibly of the excellent reasons why she was now a level-headed career woman rather than the dreamer she had once been. She had started out as an art major—leaning toward the commercial end of the spectrum as a compromise to her father. The Spencers did not look kindly on anything that smacked of frivolity, and the colonel had found even commercial art outrageous enough. He had finally accepted it, probably due to the fact that Grace was being put through school with money left her by her maternal grandmother, and he had never needed to contribute to her education.

And then, in her second year, she had met Don, a bearded potter who played the twelve-string guitar and raised goosebumps on her skin with his husky tenor voice. Don had dreams of setting up a small business that dealt in handmade musical instruments, natural foods and high-quality crafts, including his own distinctive pots, all in a coffeehouse atmosphere. They had become friends in the first place because he had seen some of Grace's small, meticulous drawings of lichens and wildflowers and had wondered how they would transpose onto clay.

Grace was ripe for a close relationship. The middle child, she had been lost in the shuffle between her two brothers, and then, when Jill was born six years after Evan, all yellow ringlets and big, sky-blue eyes, the colonel seemed to forget he even had another daughter. They had all adored the baby, and all of them had benefited from the slight easing of the harsh discipline in the Spencer household. As the years went by, with Colonel Spencer engrossed in his youngest child, his sons and his Civil Defense activities, Grace no longer crept through the house, afraid her father would appear suddenly around a corner to demand that she recite the seventh line of multiplication tables or threaten her with shoulder braces if she didn't straighten up.

She had been content to drift through her high school years, daydreaming, drawing and writing bad poetry. There had been occasional dates, but her father catechized her high school friends so severely before he allowed them to take her out that few of them returned for a second drilling. Bart had sometimes brought home a friend from school who took her out, but no sparks had been struck. None, that was, until Don Franklin had noticed her.

Even now she was torn between anger and embarrassment when she thought of how incredibly green she had been. Don had easily persuaded her that he wanted nothing so much as to set them both up in a cozy little business. They could live together, love together, for the rest of their natural days; working together they could build a fine business that would in no way compromise their stand against the so-called Establishment.

It had worked for eight months. She had been held spellbound by Don's seductive eyes and compelling voice and had all but dropped out of school, pouring all her energies into their joint project. The bulk of her inheritance had gone into it as well, and when she had told her family she was considering moving into Don's apartment in the back of the shabby old house they had rented for the store they had named The Apple Barrel, it had been the last straw. There had been a horrendous scene, and she had been told that she was no longer her father's daughter. Her mother, dressed to the hilt for one of her volunteer meetings, had stood by silently, supporting neither her husband nor her daughter. As Grace had driven away, biting her lip to still her quivering chin, it had occurred to her sadly that her mother had probably been too busy mulling over the program for her meeting to have heard a word.

How *could* she have been so incredibly naive? It went beyond naiveté—it was plain stupid!

Disenchantment had come slowly, insidiously, and then there had come that nightmare week when all her balloons had burst. She had discovered that Don was spending a lot of time with another girl. Strictly business, he assured her—only Don took to spending whole weekends away from the store and had stopped talking about a lovely homemade wedding in the spring, with fiddles and flutes, cheeses and mead and home-baked breads. By the time the bills started pouring in, he had disappeared altogether. Grace, who knew more about nuclear physics than she did about bookkeeping, had suddenly found herself responsible for all the debts

Don was supposed to have paid with the money she had given him. When she attempted to salvage something from the wreckage, she discovered that everything, including the secondhand van they had bought, was in Don's name. The crowning blow had come when she had returned from a painful visit—an attempted visit would be more accurate—to her family, to find that in her absence Don had taken the van and everything of any value in the store, leaving her with only the consignment goods and a mountain of debts and legal entanglements.

"Movies tomorrow night?" Elliot inquired, rousing her from a miasma of painful memories.

They were in the teachers' lounge, sipping weak coffee from the machine, and everyone had left but Grace and the math teacher, Elliot Rand. Grace shook off the past and manufactured a smile for the handsome, tweedy brunet. Elliot was nice. Dull, predictable, but extremely nice. More than once she had had to clamp down on her unfortunate penchant for doggerel when she found herself silently rhyming "Rand" with "bland."

"All right—fine. Would you like to come by for dinner first?" Now and then she tried to repay him by inviting him for a meal, for he was the sort who'd be threatened if a woman suggested paying her own way.

Elliot's hesitation was fleeting, but Grace grimaced. She was an ambitious cook—and, unfortunately, a bad one as often as not. A good bit of her creativity spilled over into culinary channels, and she could never content herself with meekly following someone else's recipe. However, all too often her concoctions were a disastrous combination of the health food she had grown accustomed to with Don, the economy fare of the subsequent years when she had worked to pay back her debts and then to put herself through business school and the mouth-watering southern dishes she had learned to love since coming to Georgia.

They compromised on Elliot's picking up fried chicken and Grace's baking potatoes and tossing a salad. To ease her nebulous sense of guilt she promised him his favorite dessert. "I'll get some butter pecan ice cream, too."

On Friday she was late getting away. In the interests of economy she usually walked to school in all but the worst weather. Today she had forgotten that Elliot would be coming at six and she had to detour by the grocery store and then walk the mile and a quarter home. With luck she'd just make it, although they might have to settle for a later film or skip it altogether. Elliot, who lived with his mother and a widowed sister in an eminently respectable part of town, liked to dine at six on the nose, and they usually made the seven o'clock feature. That way he was home before his womenfolk could begin to worry. Dull, predictable and, let's face it, Grace—nonthreatening. For all his almost too perfect features and his manly pipe and tweeds, he didn't make her heart beat one whit faster, and that was precisely why she continued to date him.

If she hadn't been running late, she wouldn't have been in a hurry, and if she hadn't been in a hurry, she wouldn't have been racing when she left the grocer's with fresh spinach and ice cream. And if she hadn't been racing, she wouldn't have barged into that man.

"Ouch!" Her hair caught in a button on his work-stained khaki shirt and she jumped back, snagging several strands, and sidestepped, glaring up into the familiar face. No hard hat today—just the Mephistophelian arches over warmly amused eyes, the broad grin that creased the lean cheeks into what might have been called dimples in a lesser man.

Unfortunately he sidestepped, too, and in the same

direction. They both dodged again, and Grace swore in frustrated irritation. Before she could avoid his hamlike hands, they had clasped her elbows and lifted her, groceries and all, swinging her to one side and then lowering her gently back to the pavement. Then he bowed his head in mock servility and strode away, leaving Grace feeling as though she had been plowed under by the bulldozer he handled so skillfully.

The potatoes were underdone, and to make it worse Elliot rather ostentatiously ignored it, except for an oblique comment. "You shouldn't walk when you have a schedule to keep, Grace. Especially with a bag of groceries and a briefcase as well as your purse to carry."

Grace frowned as something tugged at the edges of her mind. "My briefcase!" She jumped up from the table, pulling the cloth and rattling the cups in their saucers as she raced into the front room. Her briefcase was not on the plant-filled table where she always slung it when she came in. Nor was it on her bed or anywhere else.

"What's wrong?" Elliot glanced surreptitiously at his watch, reminding her that they were getting off schedule.

"Oh, nothing, really. It's just that I forgot my briefcase, darn it! And it's Friday."

"If it's important we could run by and pick it up," he offered grudgingly, and Grace shook herself out of her mood and smiled at him. He really *was* kind, and she was being silly, but her briefcase was a sort of security blanket. In it she carried all her drawing and writing paraphernalia, including the notebook in which she scribbled ideas for new verses as they occurred to her. There was almost a month's accumulation of new work, all ready to be transcribed and mailed off to Mr. Harris, and all her drawings, including a rather intricate design of palmetto whorls and one of flower faces she had been working on in her spare time.

"Oh, it's not important. Just the usual batch of papers, and I can do without them until Monday." Elliot didn't know about her sideline. For reasons that escaped her, she had told no one of the foolishly romantic little verses and the whimsical drawings she had been selling for several years. "Let's put the dishes in to soak and I'll do them after I get home tonight. Are we going to see the Clint Eastwood thing?"

Elliot's rather full lips thinned in disapproval. He disapproved of a lot of things, including Grace's home and her neighborhood. "If you want to, of course, but they're showing *Patton* again and I rather thought . . ."

"Sure. Fine. I love the part when he's on an ancient battlefield and he recalls a past life. The music . . ." She trailed off, unwilling to invite a lecture on the *true* value of the film. Elliot's favorites tended to be rather violent, which was surprising in someone otherwise so meek and conservative.

On Monday she raced to school to find her briefcase. It was not where she thought she had left it, but she located it on the table beside the copying machine and breathed a sigh of relief. She tucked it safely under her desk, then went over her roster and determined which girls would be assigned to which machines for the nine o'clock class. Horace MacCready, or at least his trustees, had certainly endowed the school to the hilt when it came to equipping it with all the latest in business machines. Not surprising when one considered that the original MacCready fortune had come from the early patents on some of them.

QD and company was out in full force today, and the men—some of them were hardly more than boys—

were performing in fine style. Grace recalled someone's mentioning that most of them were co-op students from Georgia Tech. Maybe she should borrow a leaf from the military and bark out, "Eyes *right!*" If it wasn't an admission of her utter failure as a disciplinarian, she would have covered the windows. Instead she tried to ignore the swarming men and the whispering, distracted girls and plowed on with her lecture on interfacing terminals. Boring. She caught herself in a sigh and her glance slipped sideways through the wall of glass.

Suddenly it seemed that everywhere she went, she was confronted by that immense, curly-headed creature with the outrageously fresh grin. Crossing the campus to the parking lot, she saw him standing beside one of the blue QD trucks, talking to several men. He veered off, tossing them a casual salute as she neared, and swung into step beside her. "Afternoon, Pigtails. If you're going to the grocer's again, it's on my way."

"I'm not," she snapped smartly. Then a grudging "Thank you." She killed a crazy impulse to reach up and assure herself that her neat chignon was still intact. It was only at home, or when she was out in the field by herself, that she wore it in a braid—and wouldn't you know he'd have noticed! At least it hadn't been streaming down her back. She had worn her hair down in the old days, but for years now she had felt particularly vulnerable unless it was securely knotted or braided.

"How about a lift home? Or do you live on campus?" he asked, one of those wicked brows lifting questioningly.

"No thank you and no." Staring straight ahead, Grace blessed the providence that had made her wear her dark-brown tailored suit and the plain white blouse today. Her hair was neatly confined, her makeup nonexistent, and the nearest thing to a scent she could be accused of wearing was the herbal fragrance soap and talc she used. She walked briskly, her posture erect enough to have brought a gleam of approval from the colonel himself. Beside her the hard-hatted, khaki-clad giant swung easily, his enormous booted feet making her tan calf size-fives look like doll's feet.

"You look like you've had a tough day. Why don't you let me buy you a beer on the way home?" His soft Georgia drawl flowed over her like warm molasses, and she fancied she could feel the heat radiating from his virile body.

She turned to confront him, her brows leveled and her expression forbidding. "Look, would you please just leave me alone? I *don't* need a ride, I *don't* want your company and I *don't* drink beer!"

The smile that warmed his eyes and revealed his strong, white teeth in no way softened the weathered planes of his face. She noted irrelevantly that his thick, brushy mustache was actually as carefully groomed as the hair that curled so incongruously from beneath his metal hat. He said, "Did you know your eyes are the exact color of lapis lazuli?"

Feeling oddly as if she were walking down an up escalator, she stared at him for several long moments before she remembered to scowl again. What color *was* lapis lazuli? If she ever knew, she had forgotten, but be darned if she'd ask!

He reached out one hand and touched her neat, businesslike chignon. "If you used a wrench, you could probably tighten up another half turn on this thing, but then I guess your ears really *would* stick out." Before she could react, he sauntered off, a casual "See you" tossed over his massive shoulder.

She stood there blinking after him, one hand straying up to flutter against her small, flat ear. Once again she had allowed that aggravating creature to short-circuit her thinking processes! What *was* it about him? A beer, indeed! Belly up to the bar, boys! Did she look like the sort of woman who stopped off at the local bar for a beer on her way home?

As she strolled through the damp, chilly evening, ignoring the traffic that flowed past her, she wondered if she wasn't making too much of the whole thing. She could have taken him up on it. Just because she had never cultivated a taste for beer didn't mean she had to turn up her nose at his invitation. Face it, it wasn't the specific invitation that had made her overreact, but the man himself. He was too big, too tough, too uncouth, too—too *everything!* She closed her mind quickly to the small voice that whispered he was also too attractive. Dangerously so. She *would* be an awful fool if she took to mooning around over a mustache and a pair of shoulders broad enough to bear the woes of the world. She'd be no better than that classroom full of impressionable girls whose greedy little faces followed his monstrous bulldozer the way a sunflower followed the sun. Her life was very well ordered without *that* particular complication. She had her career, her house, her plants and her cats, plus a hobby that afforded her not only pleasure and satisfaction, but a few dollars as well.

And Elliot. Don't forget Elliot. He had invited her to church and dinner with him and his mother next Sunday, and she had put him off. He had told her once that his mother considered her a nice, sensible young woman, and she had thought at the time, how unspeakably dull I sound! Was she really that bad? She grinned ruefully. Wouldn't it be ironic if her closest social tie were based on mutual boredom?

A cold front dropped down into the Southeast unexpectedly on Friday, and Grace bundled up and ran the gamut of cats out as far as the road. "Rats," she muttered, bemoaning the thinning of her good Yankee blood. She turned and hurried back to where her car was pulled up beside the house. There was no point in being foolish about it—being laid up with the flu would cost her more than a few pints of gas. She was just a couple of blocks from school when the tire blew. No warning at all, just a loud explosion that startled her out of her wits.

She wrestled with the steering wheel and managed to pull off the highway and then she just sat there, fingers drumming on the steering wheel in frustration. It had been a practically new recap, too, meant to last until spring, when she had budgeted for recapping two more tires and rotating them. With an exasperated grunt she slammed out and began searching in the trunk for the various parts of equipment needed to change the thing. At least her spare was up.

The bumper jack adjusted, she had it cranked almost high enough to clear the ground when the blue pickup slowed and pulled in behind her. She didn't even have to raise her head to know who it was; the prickling at the back of her neck was enough to alert her. Twice in the past week she had almost run into the genial giant, and once she had crossed the street just to avoid him. If she didn't know better, she might have suspected he was deliberately following her. Brunswick was a small town, but not that small!

"Having a little trouble, Pigtails?"

"Not at all," she said chillingly. She pried off the hubcap, glared at the lug wrench, determined which end fit the nuts and tackled the first one. It wouldn't budge.

"Be glad to offer you a hand, ma'am," the man drawled softly. He was standing some five feet away, one booted foot crossed over the other, with his fists bracing his narrow hips.

Forcing herself not to rush, Grace found a nut she could loosen and then moved on to the next one. "I'm perfectly capable of changing a tire. Thank you for your offer, but I don't need any help." She jolted the wrench furiously in an effort to unfreeze the stubborn lug, and even as she stifled a Marine Corp-strength oath, she heard the slam of a door, the growl of eight cylinders, and the truck drove slowly past her before resuming normal speed.

She got help from a couple of high school boys who gladly accepted the two dollars she handed them, and was only twenty minutes late for her first class.

From there the day went downhill. Terri expressed her hostility toward the word processor by ramming in a systems disc at an angle and damaging it beyond further use. "I *hate* a machine that argues with me and then won't listen to me when I argue back!"

Inwardly Grace sympathized. She had had a wretched time with all the complex systems she had had to master. In fact, she had had a wretched time in every single one of her classes, with Elementary Business Law leading the pack. Thank goodness she didn't have to teach *that* class! She had taken it, though, for the same reason she had struggled through all the rest. No man was going to take advantage of her in *any* way in the future. Never again would she carry a marshmallow heart where her brain ought to be. When she learned a lesson, she learned it all the way!

Elliot complained about everything on his plate at lunch, and finally, over a peach cobbler Grace found delicious, he told her that someone had stuck a decal on his brand-new, gold-monogrammed briefcase.

"Oh, Elliot, no! Did you try to get it off?" She had

been amused at his blatant pride in the expensive bit of luggage, especially as he had managed to tell her several times what it had cost him, not including the gold initials, but his very real distress made her ashamed of herself. "I could try, if you'd like. Maybe if we soak it a bit?"

He seemed slightly mollified. "I'm going to take it to the leather shop this afternoon. I've already talked to Mr. Small about it. Those horrible juvenile delinquents! It's not the first time they've done something like this, you know. How you've managed to escape I'll never know, because you've got that same high school bunch I've got for three classes! Absolutely no breeding!"

The day finally ended and Grace walked to the parking lot with Elliot, murmuring something sufficiently sympathetic when he showed her the slightly risque version of the familiar Happy Day face that was plastered on the polished leather. They made plans for dinner and a program on television the following night, and Grace mentioned having to get something done about her tire, and then they parted beside Elliot's three-year-old white Ford.

The phone was ringing when she let herself in and she groaned. With her luck it would be either the dentist reminding her of an appointment or the IRS inviting her for an audit.

It was neither. To her delight it was the president of All Seasons Greeting Cards, Inc., congratulating her on their joint success. The entry Mr. Harris had selected for the annual competition had been one of Grace's valentine designs, both artwork and verse, and it had won first place! "That's two hundred and fifty dollars, Grace, and you get half of it as well as the fancy blue ribbon. I'll put it in the mail tomorrow."

"You've made my day, Mr. Harris—my whole week. In fact, my whole year!" Elated, she rattled on until Claude Harris pleaded another call, and then she sat there, hands clasped tightly in her lap, and grinned at the bilbergia that was just now sending up its red flower stems to be ready for a Christmas blooming. One of the cats had managed to get in when she raced for the phone and she scooped her up, crowing, "Did you hear that, Miss Maudie? I'm the best in the country! The best in the world, for all I know!" A slight, forgivable exaggeration. The larger firms didn't even bother to enter, as the organization was comprised mostly of smaller outfits that relied completely on free-lance work, but anyway, she was better than *some*one at *some*thing!

She dialed swiftly, then listened to the distant *burr, burr,* picturing the austere blue, gray and white foyer of her parents' house. They'd be horrified if they could see the rickety lime-green house she lived in. The green paint had been her uncle's idea. He had told her that Aldonia had always liked green houses, but she had no idea just how green her uncle's idea of green was.

The colonel answered, his voice a testy growl. "Yes, yes, who is it?"

"Daddy, it's me—Grace."

"I'll get your mother." Before she could protest, he was gone. She'd have liked to tell him about her small triumph, having had so few to share with him over the years. He came back on the line and she started to speak, but he interrupted her. "Your mother's with her board members. Some silly new female cause she's got herself mixed up with. She'll call you later, and now, if there's nothing else, I'm late for my own meeting. I'm being named Citizen of the Year tonight. I'll send you a clipping."

Whee! Aren't we Spencers fantastic? she crowed silently as she slowly placed the phone in its cradle. Dismissing the momentary blight her parents' lack of interest had created, she lifted the receiver and dialed again. The phone rang and rang, and finally she gave up. Bart was evidently out. She tried Evan and got Janice, his wife, who proceeded to pour out her dissatisfaction with the quality of the carpet they had just installed, and then launched an attack against a company that had sold them a dishwasher and made such a terrible mess of installing it that the thing had never worked right.

With no feeling of compunction at all, Grace hung up on her sister-in-law, mid-squawk. Janice had never been satisfied with anything in her life, and Grace was very much afraid that included poor Evan. She turned to the cat, who was contentedly curling her claws in and out of a crewel-embroidered pillow. "Have you heard the big news, Miss Maudie? One of my designs won a top national contest and I'm to be awarded the phenomenal sum of one hundred and twenty-five smackeroos, not to mention one genuine rayon satin rosette, the likes of which you have never seen!" She turned to the bilbergia and its companions, an absurdly overgrown angelwing begonia, a hindu rope plant and a collection of anonymous succulents, and said, "You heard that, didn't you? That means an extra serving of plant food for each one of you, and what's more I might—no promises, mind you—but I just might see my way clear to get you that special light you've been begging me for. We'll see," she finished airily.

Briefly she considered calling Jill and dismissed it as the edge went off her pleasure. It wasn't really all *that* earthshaking. At least, not to anyone outside her own immediate household. She opened the door and put Miss Maudie outside to join her friends and relatives. "See you on the side porch, girls," she said tiredly. "You can finish off that bouillabaisse I made night before last. The cloves were a mistake, I think."

Chapter Three

A dismal gray rain was drumming down on the metal roof when Grace woke up on Saturday morning. She expertly loaded the seldom-used woodstove and struck a match to the paper. The baseboard in the kitchen was already damp when she went in to put on a pot of coffee, and she decided to hurry and get her bath before the water rose any higher. The bathroom always sunk first.

It was absurd in this day and age for anyone to live in such a place! Back when Henry and Aldonia had rented the old house, four rooms and a *path* had been the order of the day. Somewhere along the line the owner had generously tacked on a rudimentary bathroom by closing in a corner of what had been a back porch, but the house was at least sixty years old and it had been slowly sinking into the ground all those years. Half a mile or so in either direction fancy new homes were going up, and Grace feared for her small, private domain. The privacy, along with the view of the marshes, was one of the most appealing things about the place. That, plus the fact that even in its genteel shabbiness, the little frame house had a warmth that she had never found in any of her previous homes. Not the military housing on the various bases, nor the big square two-story house her father had bought after he retired, nor the two sparsely furnished rooms she had lived in while she worked to put herself through business school.

Maybe it was the luxuriant and overflowing plants, Great-aunt Aldonia's beloved collection or the cats that populated the yard and the porches. Even the inconvenient old woodstove added to the coziness, with its copper kettle and an occasional pot of chowder simmering on top in the winter.   Heating with wood had its drawbacks, but she had come to enjoy it, especially as the Georgia winters were usually mild.

Still, something was going to have to be done or the back part of the house was going to float off down the Back River one of these fine days. Without waiting to eat breakfast, she dialed the agent who handled the property and outlined her situation succinctly, letting him know that if something wasn't done about it immediately, she'd be forced to contact the authorities. Just which authorities, she couldn't have said, but her threat was evidently enough to stir the rental agent into action.

"You understand, Miss Spencer, that the property you rent for next to nothing should have been condemned years ago. We allowed your relatives to go on living there because they couldn't afford anything else, and the only reason we let you continue on the same lease is that the owner hasn't gotten around to doing anything else with that particular tract. It's a valuable property, Miss Spencer, and sooner or later the whole area will be cleared for development."

"Well, meanwhile, Mr. Ogleby, I'm in danger of washing away. There's already water seeping into the kitchen, and there's half an inch all over the bathroom floor. There's no heat out there except for an electric heater, and needless to say, I can't use that under these conditions. How would you and your wife like . . ."

"Yes, well, all right, Miss Spencer, I'll see if the owner wants to bother with fixing it up, but I wouldn't hold out much hope if I were you."

"Now," she insisted, and he repeated "Now" in resignation before hanging up.

Now would probably be sometime next week, she fumed as she made herself some breakfast and took it into the back living room. She had probably cooked her own goose. Monday she'd better start looking around for inexpensive housing, but nothing would suit her as well as this place did, garish paint, woodstove, subterranean bathroom and all.

Curling her feet under her on the sofa, she snapped open her briefcase and took out the sheaf of original verses that had accumulated over the past year. As a rule she didn't mind gloomy weather, but for some reason she was feeling dismal today. A little harmless gloating might lift her spirits.

The verses were separated into batches, according to type. She submitted word-processed editions to accompany her carefully rendered illustrations on Bristol Board, but she retained the original verses, handwritten on lined paper, initialed with the tiny "GBS," and the field drawings, all carefully coded as to which went with which.

They were supposed to be in order, but they weren't. At least not in the order in which she thought she had left them. Where was that—here it was! Upside down and in the wrong batch! Just when had she been so careless?

The delicate, old-fashioned drawing she had done for the prize-winning valentine had a nineteenth-century sort of charm, an effect she had worked hard to achieve. She studied the pen and wash drawing of pink roses, tiny wild irises and forget-me-nots that formed a heart shape that had been edged with paper lace, then sorted through the verses until she found the right one. It was unabashedly sentimental—but then, that was the nature of valentines. She quoted softly from memory:

> *"Rose pink are your lips, my love,*
> *Iris blue, your eyes.*
> *Forget-me-not, for in your hands*
> *My happiness yet lies."*

Oh, it was sweet—saccharine, even. She had done mostly friendship cards at first before tackling the more traditional greetings, and it had been just after Don Franklin had left her that she had been asked to do her first valentine.

That had been ironic. A more cynical antiromantic would have been hard to find. She had done it, though. And through the years she had done more, and it grew easier each year. She told herself she was openly mocking her own foolish vulnerability—the vulnerabilities of anyone who dared believe in a hearts-and-flowers notion of True Love, and most of the time she believed it.

The final irony was to have won an award for any such drivel. She studied the drawings again, finding no criticism of her botanically accurate renditions of the blossoms. It really was rather lovely. One didn't have to believe in forget-me-nots and hearts and flowers to appreciate it—as long as one didn't open it up to read that blatantly sentimental verse.

She read through several more of her verses, finding she had actually, over the years, done far more of the sentimental sort than she had realized. Perhaps it was just because her delicate drawings of wildflowers lent themselves to the theme.

Feeling the beginnings of a burst of creative energy, she uncapped her fountain pen and stared at the window shelf of flowing, draping, climbing houseplants and waited for the muse to descend. She always did her best work outdoors, surrounded by living, growing things, and the houseplants were a poor substitute. She jumped up impulsively and opened the side door to let the cats in. Usually she kept them out because they were lethal to her plants, but today she needed the feeling of warm creatures around her.

By noon the rain had slackened and a watery, lemon-colored sun timidly fingered the trailing clouds. Grace munched a salad in which she had mixed left-overs with raw vegetables. It had been another of her mistakes, and she found it necessary to drown the concoction in salad dressing in order to finish it. She was tempted to ask Elliot to take her somewhere special tonight. She didn't have to have any particular reason for wanting to go somewhere new and different. He wouldn't have to know that it was in the order of a celebration. Actually she might even tell him about her sideline one of these days, just for the look on his face. Elliot considered her the most pragmatic of women, a quality he found admirable above all.

She was poking through her dresses, wondering what she had that could be considered festive, when she heard a vehicle drive into the yard and cut the engine. Her bedroom was on the opposite side of the house from the shelled driveway, and she dropped the lavender georgette dress she had worn to Evan's wedding and frowned. It was probably the meter reader, although she usually came during the week.

The whole house registered the heavy footsteps crossing the front porch, and by the time the screened door rattled under a summoning fist, Grace was already there, a feeling of numbed certainty creeping over her.

"What are you doing here? What do you want? How did you know where I live?" She held the door open a cautious six inches as she peered through at the man outside. The hard hat was missing and instead he held a battered Stetson in his hand as he leaned with one arm against the side of her house.

"Do you want 'em in order of importance or as issued?" he drawled laconically. Once more that ever-ready grin split his craggy features. For some reason Grace found his unshakable good humor extremely irritating.

"What do you want?" she demanded shortly. It was hard to ignore all that blatant masculinity, which irritated her further.

He leaned away from the wall and assumed a deferential attitude, the broad-brimmed hat held in front of him with both hands. "I've come to fix your plumbing, Miss Spencer," he told her with a suspicious gleam in his chocolate-dark eyes. Something about the way those appreciative eyes moved over her made her uncomfortably conscious of the fact that her newly shampooed hair was still unconfined, and the knit shirt and faded jeans clung far too faithfully to her body.

"There's nothing wrong with my plumbing," she informed him curtly. "It's the whole blasted bathroom and kitchen—the floors are too low! And anyhow, what are you doing here? It's certainly not a bulldozer job, and how did you know my name, anyway?"

He held up a staying hand, and Grace tried not to be so aware of the long, sculptured fingers, the smooth calluses on the oversized palm. "One at a time, Pigtails. You sure do rattle on, don't you?"

"My name is *not* Pigtails! Who are you, anyway? What do you plan to do about my flooding problem?"

"Yes, ma'am, Miss Spencer, I read you loud and clear. As a matter of fact, I think—"

"I'm not interested in what you think, Mister . . ."

"Donovan, Miss Spencer, and in case you wondered, Ogleby sent me."

Just for an instant there was a gleam of something that struck her oddly in those dark, enigmatic eyes, and then it was gone. He was merely a workman, hat in hand, with a deferential smile that just happened to be rather more attractive than most.

"All right, Mr. Donovan. The problem is easy enough to recognize if you'll just go on around to the back. I'll be inside if you should need anything, but I expect you have whatever tools you'll need. Oh, one thing," she added before closing the door in his face. "Do I pay you or do you deal with the owner of the property? Mr. Ogleby didn't say, and frankly, your chances of collecting your wages from the skinflint who owns this place are pretty dim." She tried to ignore the way the man's eyes moved appreciatively over her hair, her face, dropping slowly down the length of her long throat to linger on the yellow knit shirt. That sort of man would ogle anything female—as she had good cause to know, after two months of watching the disgusting byplay between her girls and his men!

Her lips tightened ominously. "Send your bill to the rental agency, if you don't mind. I promise you, if Mr. Ogleby can't collect from the owner, I'll be glad to pay your going rate." She closed the door firmly and leaned back against it, blowing a strand of hair off her fore-

head. Whew! At close quarters the man was unbelievable! In spite of all the years of fasting since Don had
swept her off her feet and then hurled her back to earth
again, she felt the old half-forgotten hungers begin to
stir deep inside her.

It was no good. Pacing from room to room, she had
picked up and cleaned up everything in sight in an
effort to work off some of her restlessness. She had left
the print of her brow on every window in the house as
she stared out at the sodden countryside. The steady
thuds as shovelsful of wet dirt being thrown aside were
as inescapable as her own heartbeat.

The phone rang as she was tugging on her rubber
boots, and she answered it to hear Elliot confirming
their date. He was the only man she had ever known
who was so punctilious. "Elliot, I'd really like to go to
that new place over on Lanier Island. I've heard they
have a band on Saturday nights, and I haven't danced
in years!" She left the next step up to him, listening
with growing amusement as the silence lengthened. She
could picture his expression as his brain clicked out the
probable cost of such an evening. "Elliot? Why don't
we make it my party? I'm expecting a—a dividend in a
few days, and I'd really like to treat you."

The sound of a clearing throat came over the line. I
also have a tire to get mended and a drainage ditch to
pay for, she reminded herself.

"That won't be necessary, Grace. If you'd like to go
there, of course I'll take you—that is, if I can get
reservations this late," he added hopefully—hoping he
couldn't, and would have a good excuse to return to
their regular restaurant at Gloucester and Bay where,
according to him, the stewed chicken and dumplings
was always a safe bet.

It occurred to her that even on a beer and hamburger

budget, the man called Donovan would steer clear of any place that could at best be called "safe," and then she felt a rush of guilt. Elliot asked little enough of her on their weekly dates—just a sympathetic ear for his indignation over the practical jokes his students played on him, and an occasional murmur as he recited his mother's opinions on just about everything. Even his good-night kiss asked nothing of her—which was all on the plus side, wasn't it? He was a fine man and probably a very good business math instructor, even if he lacked a sense of humor.

And anyway, a man like Donovan probably made more in a day than she or Elliot did in a week. Skilled heavy-equipment operators were rather more highly paid than low-seniority schoolteachers. If anyone should be moonlighting as a handy man, it should be Elliot, although she couldn't picture him rolling up his sleeves and pitching into anything more strenuous than pushing the buttons on a calculator.

She stuffed her foot into her other boot, then pulled on a bulky wool sweater and collected her portfolio. She chased the last cat out and stepped out the back door. Donovan had stripped off his shirt, and with each movement of those brawny arms as he deepened the canal that led away from her house, his powerful muscles gleamed in the pale sunlight. Humidity had tightened the black curls above those dramatic gray sideburns, and his eyes flashed a greeting at her as he continued to work without breaking stride.

"I'm leaving," she called out.

"Sure. How about leaving the back door open for me? I'll lock up when I'm done." Once more his eyes seemed to envelop her slender form in genial appreciation.

Disconcerted, she hesitated. Give a man like that the

run of her house? She'd just as soon invite a wild buffalo inside! "If you want to wash up when you're finished, there's a faucet around on the side."

"Thanks, but how about leaving the back door unlocked, anyway, hmmm?"

Her suspicions clearly evident, she eyed him doubtfully, and he told her he needed to check the flooring in the two back rooms for damp rot.

"Oh—of course." Her relief might have been construed as insulting, and she hastened to say, "Just send your bill to Mr. Ogleby. I'll see that you're paid within—two weeks? Will that be soon enough?" May as well give the owner a chance to cough up, just in case his guilty conscience overcame his stinginess.

Donovan leaned on his shovel and wiped a hand across his wet brow. Even in early December it could be hot when you were shoveling wet dirt.

"Would you like something cold to drink?" compunction made her inquire.

"You wouldn't have a beer, would you?"

"I'm afraid not. Milk? Orange juice?"

"You know, what I'd really enjoy is a cup of hot coffee. I don't suppose . . . ?" His eyes were softly wistful as he let the words dangle between them, and Grace had no option. With a sigh she nodded and turned to go back into the kitchen. "I'll just step in here and clean up a bit," he said from two steps behind her. The bathroom and kitchen doors were only a few feet apart across a tiny vestibule that was all that was left of the back porch. "I'll take a look around at the same time. Probably need to replace the whole floor from the joists up with treated lumber."

She gave up. The idea of that big ox blundering around in her five-by-five-foot bathroom didn't bear dwelling on. Her talc, her soap, her peach-colored towels—even her white cotton pajamas, blast it! She had a subliminal vision of his large tanned hands touching her intimate personal belongings, and it brought a distinctly hollow feeling to her middle.

The kettle, moved from the still-warm woodstove to the range, was coming to a boil when he appeared in the kitchen, almost filling the opening. With a strangely unsteady hand Grace poured the boiling water through the filter and took a deep breath, determined to ignore him while she waited for the water to settle so that she could pour the rest.

He removed the kettle gently from her hand. "Why don't you get the cups and saucers out while I do this? How many did you make?"

"One," she said deliberately, not daring to lift her eyes to his disturbing nearness.

"Then I'll just add a little more and make it two. I never liked to drink alone."

Taking a deep, steadying breath, Grace reached down two small mugs. They were some Don had made and she had decorated with an incised design of fern fronds before they were fired. She may as well give in peaceably, because it was impossible to argue with such a creature. How long could it take to finish off one small serving of coffee, anyway?

He led her into the living room, and she noticed for the first time that he had removed his boots before coming inside. Even without them he threatened the ceiling fixture as he passed under it on his way across the room. Just as if he had every right, he opened the door of her woodstove and peered inside, then shook down the smoldering ashes before closing the door and settling himself on her sofa. Talk about making yourself at home!

"When's the last time you had your chimney inspected?"

Thrown off base by the unexpected question, Grace

stared at him blankly. "My—why . . . I suppose Uncle Henry had it done." She was sitting on the edge of a straight chair, hoping that her precarious perch would give him the idea that she wasn't about to settle down for a cozy visit.

"I'll send someone out next week," he said, his soft baritone drawl almost distracting her from his outrageous presumptuousness.

"Look, I'm sure you mean well, Mr. Donovan, but . . ."

"Call me Quinn."

"*Mr. Donovan,*" she stressed determinedly, "but if I need a handyman, I'm sure Mr. Ogleby can find—"

"Clark Ogleby couldn't find his glasses if they were on top of his head. There's a man who specializes in these old unlined chimneys and he can clean the thing out for you while he's here. And I'll bet you haven't had that done, either, have you?" he taunted with his good-natured grin. How could any man be so . . . so impossibly *pleasant!*

"Well, thank you very much, Mr. Donovan. If you're finished with your coffee . . . ?" She stood and waited expectantly for him to do the same thing. Instead he leaned back on her granny afghan and smiled sweetly up at her, his powerfully muscled legs extended in front of him.

"There's a new supper club that's opened up over on Lanier Island. How'd you like to try it out tonight?"

She removed a withered leaf from one of the begonias and said cautiously, "I've heard about it. It's supposed to have a marvelous band on weekends." She watched his eyes warm with anticipation and then continued, almost reluctantly, "That's why my date is taking me there tonight for dinner and dancing."

Her conscience needled her momentarily at the fleeting expression of disappointment that crossed his face, but then the familiar 220-volt smile flashed on again and she stiffened her defenses. His ego could take any harmless blows she happened to land. If her girls were any example, he was used to knocking them dead with that toothpaste ad grin and those wicked brows of his. For all she knew, he could be married and have a houseful of children. He was certainly old enough—late thirties or early forties at least. No man so loaded with all that southern-fried charm would allow a small thing like a wife to slow him down.

"Right. I thank you kindly for the coffee, ma'am. I think you were on your way somewhere, so why don't you go ahead and lock up. I'll come by some other time to finish checking out the flooring." His smile was just as wide, just as attractive, but there was a subtle difference—a hardness behind it that made Grace suddenly realize that for all his easygoing manners, here was a man who'd be dangerous to cross.

As she watched him duck out through the back door, sweeping up his mud-caked boots as he stepped out onto her pint-sized porch, it occurred to Grace to wonder why she felt such an overwhelming need to resist his friendly overtures. Certainly she wasn't snob enough to reject him because he made a living digging ditches, either with a shovel or a bulldozer?

The thing was, they'd have absolutely nothing at all in common. Donovan was the sort of man who'd want to watch football and drink beer in his sock feet on a Saturday, and she'd rather listen to a broadcast from the Met while she sipped a glass of wine. And if the weather was fine, she'd want to ramble through the woods and maybe linger to write or sketch, while he'd be out somewhere fishing or gunning down helpless birds.

She snatched up her portfolio, stalked across the front porch and made a wide swing around to the road, heading for her favorite haunt. She'd only have time to get there before it was time to turn around and come back again, but at least she could walk off some of this . . . this nervous energy that seethed inside her.

And besides, she argued with herself as thoughts of the genial Donovan dogged her marching feet along the puddled road, he had only suggested taking her out to dinner—not a lifetime of love in a cottage!

Elliot was precisely on time, as usual, and Grace greeted him at the door wearing the lavender georgette, with her hair, for once, swirling around her shoulders. She had used a touch of coral lipstick and a hint of eye shadow, an unusual departure for her. Her eyes—what color *was* lapis lazuli, anyway? She had meant to look it up. Her eyes, a dark opaque blue shot with tiny flakes of gold, gleamed with an uncharacteristic intensity, and Elliot looked thoroughly taken aback.

"Grace? Am I too early?"

"Of course not, Elliot." Elliot hated unpunctuality and she never made him wait.

"You haven't fixed your hair," he mumbled, looking almost embarrassed by the unusually frivolous style. For Pete's sake, did he think women these days only took down their hair in the privacy of their boudoir? Maybe she had been overdoing the coolheaded businesswoman image.

"I thought I'd just leave it down for a change, but if it bothers you . . . ?"

"No—I—no, that is . . . I'll help you with your wrap."

The servicable brown. Hardly the thing to wear over lavender georgette, but coats cost money and hers had been spent on more practical items. The georgette, bought for her brother's wedding, was bias cut on simple lines that skimmed her body to swirl flatteringly around her knees. The style was timeless and she adored the color, which was somewhere between wild iris and forget-me-not blue.

The supper club was crowded and she smiled warmly at Elliot and thanked him for bringing her. He could easily have begged off and claimed he couldn't get reservations. She caught a glimpse of them both in a mirror as they made their way to the table and was startled at the attractive sight they presented. Elliot really was extremely handsome in his pinstriped suit and black knit tie, and she hardly recognized the slender girl in the short, swirling dress and the flowing, leaf-brown hair. The shoes that went with the dress were a shade darker, a matter of a few spaghetti straps and tall, thin heels that flattered her small feet, and she felt her walk take on an added verve. She had forgotten how it felt to be attractive and to sense the looks of speculation and appreciation from masculine eyes.

Not Elliot's, of course. To her amusement, he was still slightly disapproving of her metamorphosis. After all, what would Mother think?

She ordered from the right-hand side of the menu, selecting the least expensive entree, and sipped her modestly priced white wine as she watched the dancers. Her foot tapped unconsciously.

"Would you care to dance?" Elliot asked resignedly. He rose to the occasion beautifully, almost disguising the fact that he didn't care for dancing, and Grace soon loosened up and enjoyed herself. They were on their second dance and Elliot had just suggested that they make their way back to the table before their meal was served when Grace spied a broad back and a familiar set of shoulders. There was no mistaking the crop of dark curls, nor could she miss the slender, silver-tipped fingers that were reaching around his shoulder to tease the strip of tanned skin that showed between the black curls and the pristine shirt.

Grace led the way back to their table, glad of Elliot's stocky form between her and Donovan's back. She was dismayed to realize that her heart was beating far too rapidly, nor could she blame it on the mild exertion of dancing to a slow, romantic ballad.

More dismaying still, she wasn't all that shocked to see him there. It was almost as if she had been expecting him. Hadn't there been a thread of subliminal excitement bubbling just under the surface the whole time she had been dressing? How long had it been since she had used makeup and worn her hair long? She knew full well that Elliot preferred her in her tailored suits and conservative shirtwaists, with her hair neatly coiled at the back of her head.

For the next half hour she divided her attention between the glittering view of dozens of moored yachts on the still water of Saint Simons Sound, and her broiled flounder, red rice and salad. Not to mention the sinfully rich fresh coconut pie. Elliot talked between courses, reminding her of his mother's invitation to Sunday dinner.

"She'd like for you to plan on spending Christmas day with us, too, Grace," he announced, and she glanced up warily, startled to see a look of slightly fatuous pride on his smooth face. "She likes you, you know."

The accolade settled over her shoulders like one of the frequent winter fogs. Suddenly she had a vision of herself being subjected to a daily firsthand account of Mother Rand's Opinions. Better the strict, barren atmosphere of her own early home life than the thinly disguised battleship tactics of that formidable woman. Grace had met her but twice and that was two times too many. Hermione Rand made the colonel seem like a flower child by comparison!

"Thanks, Elliot, but I'm planning to spend Christmas

with my family," she said gently. Actually she hadn't given a thought to her holiday plans, but suddenly she was terribly homesick. "I'm ready to leave anytime you are. I feel as if I ought to walk all the way back across the causeway to take care of that pie. It was scrumptuous!"

She saw Elliot's gaze go beyond her and up—and up and up. The baby-fine hair at the back of her neck stirred in apprehension and then Donovan's rich, deep drawl greeted her. "Did the dance band come up to your expectations, Miss Spencer?"

Moving as if she were an arthritic ninety years old, Grace turned and scowled up at him. As striking as he was in khaki work clothes, he was devastating in the flawlessly tailored dark suit and a silvery gray tie that matched the hair at his temples. Struggling against the spell of that suspiciously benign smile, Grace made sketchy introductions. "Elliot, Mr. Donovan. Mr. Donovan, Elliot Rand." Let them sort it out between them if they wanted more.

Donovan extended his hand. It brushed against Grace's shoulder and she flinched. As it enveloped Elliot's reluctantly offered one, she couldn't help but notice the contrast. Both hands were perfectly well kept, but whereas Elliot's was thin, limp and pale, Donovan's was tanned and work-honed. Grace stirred restlessly.

"Bland—glad to meet you. I won't keep y'all, but I wanted to apologize to Pigtails here for leaving such a mess in her bathroom." He turned his guileless gaze on Grace. "Next time I'll bring my own towels, honey. You folks have a good time. See you."

He was gone, weaving his way smoothly through the dancing couples. Grace stared after him, her mouth slightly agape, and watched while an auburn-haired girl with a hard sort of prettiness welcomed him back to their table. It was several moments before she turned back to Elliot, and then her eyes widened. Gone was that subtle air of self-satisfaction. In its place was one of barely concealed distaste, couple with a white-lipped anger that took her completely by surprise. "Elliot?" she ventured. Not even the abuse of his precious briefcase had generated *this* much emotion.

"And just what was *that* all about, if I may inquire?" he demanded stiffly.

"Elliot, Mr. Donovan's just the . . ."

"I *know* who Donovan is, Grace. Everybody in Glynn County knows that!" The words were more than a little contemptuous. "What I want to know is what he was doing in your—your bathroom! And just why he thinks he can address you in such a familiar manner!"

Elliot, jealous? No. It wasn't jealousy that prompted such an uncharacteristic display. His overblown sense of propriety was offended. Taking a deep breath, Grace struggled for composure against a mixture of irritation and amusement. Donovan had done that deliberately— the Pigtails bit and the oh-so-casual "honey." She should be furious with him! Oddly enough, though, she admitted to a hidden spring of amusement, along with a decided sense of relief. Elliot, of course, would go right home and relate the whole incident to his mother, who would then retract her invitations—and probably forbid her son to have any more to do with a woman who entertained strange men in her bathroom. Grace could hear her now: "She's not our kind of people, Elliot, dear. After all, a woman who lives *alone,* and in *that* neighborhood . . ."

"Forget it, Elliot. It was nothing, really." She gathered up her purse and tucked her hair back behind her ears. "I'm afraid I can't make Sunday dinner—thank your mother for me, though, will you?"

"Perhaps another time," Elliot said stiffly, escorting her out to the car. Both of them knew there would not be another time, and Grace was amazed at the feeling of lightness she felt in spite of the weight of the serviceable coat that was more suited to a Vermont spring than a South Georgia winter.

Chapter Four

December fluctuated from tropical balminess to shivering chilliness to the impenetrable fogs that could drift in so swiftly over the hundreds of square miles of marshland. Grace had still not let anyone at home know of her holiday plans. Evan and Bart lived in the same town with their parents, but Jill had been trying her luck at modeling in New York. The last time Grace had called, the youngest member of the Spencer family had been in high dudgeon because she had been cast in a television commercial as a housewife with a dyspeptic kitchen sink and the money was too good to turn down. So much for bachelor button eyes and a head full of pretty yellow curls, Grace mused in recollection. Jill had been the undisputed beauty queen of Hansonville, but then, New York City was full of small-town queens who had come to make their fortunes.

With the last of her gifts wrapped, Grace considered using as gift cards The Valentine. She had come to think of it in capitals. More than once she had been tempted to tell her family about her free-lance work, but something always stopped her—possibly the fact that she had never considered anything she had done good enough to meet their standards. Suddenly she no longer cared. She was Grace Blair Spencer, a person in her own right, and not just an extension of the family ego. She'd mail each of them one of the special valentines in February, with a note telling them about her free-lance work and the award she had won, and if they ridiculed her efforts, so what? She had shrugged off worse.

Holiday fever had set in at MCV. The discipline problem threatened to get altogether out of hand, with Terri regaling the others with exaggerated accounts of her dates . . . or perhaps they weren't exaggerated. It had been Terri—she was certain of that—who had left the X-rated book in her top drawer, and the whole room had rocked with laughter while Grace had burned, then blanched, then burned again. She simply didn't know how to deal with it. How would her father have handled insubordination, disrespect—ridicule?

That had blown over, but evidently everyone still had delicious secrets to be shared, although the tight little whispering, giggling groups dispersed readily enough when Grace approached.

They were still panting over Donovan, even though he had not been on the job for over two weeks. Most of them, she gathered, knew him by reputation if not personally. According to Carly Johns, whose father knew him, he was a Brunswick native. He was also Elvis, Burt Reynolds and Prince Charles rolled into one, and the girls seemed almost to dare Grace to deny it, eyeing her with barely suppressed excitement whenever his name was mentioned.

It was unfortunate that the library was just across the

hall. Celia Putney, the librarian, was getting to be almost as big a thorn in Grace's side as the girls. Grace carefully avoided glancing into the library whenever she left her classroom, but Celia had stopped by her table in the cafeteria more than once with a rather snide little word of warning about the noisiness of her classes—and usually in Elliot's presence, which somehow made it harder to swallow.

Grace could hardly claim it came as a surprise when she was called into the office on a Friday afternoon in the middle of December and told that unless the discipline in her morning classes improved, she was going to be given notice. Celia's doing, no doubt. The librarian hadn't even tried to disguise the malicious satisfaction on her smug face when Grace had returned to the classroom to collect her things.

Stunned, she drove slowly homeward through a spectacular sunset, oblivious to it and to the frustration of the traffic piling up behind her. The possibility of being fired had never occurred to her, although now that she thought about it, she did recall something about a probationary period. It was probably a standard part of the contract. In spite of all her business training and her hard-headed resolutions, she still hated to read the fine print.

Good Lord, wouldn't that give her family something to jeer at! When she had announced her intention of staying on in the South, they had as much as told her she wouldn't find a job, and then, when she lucked into the vacancy at MCV, they had assured her that there was more to teaching then holding the proper credentials.

It seemed they were right. Distractedly she went through the motions of checking the mailbox and feeding the cats, and then she attempted to shake herself out of her discouraged mood. After all, it was a warning, not a dismissal. All she had to do was gag and blindfold Terri and a few others. Carly Johns had actually looked embarrassed at some of Terri's more outrageous jokes at Grace's expense. Perhaps the girls would settle down after Christmas.

Searching for something to prepare for dinner, she removed a package of liver from the refrigerator—it had been on special and she had bought it impulsively, planning to disguise the flavor in a pâté. Now she boiled and mashed and chopped, throwing in handfuls of various herbs and spices, her mind still on the problem of how to blackmail her morning class into behaving. With unemployment still at a record high, it was a buyer's market, unfortunately for her.

More and more lately she had thought of her father's unbending stiffness, the ironclad rules he had imposed on his family. It was impossible to imagine him ever falling in love and marrying, much less having four children—but he had. Was it possible for people to build up such a protective mantle around themselves that it became more real than what it was meant to protect? With the perspective of several years she was able to see that her own starchiness was purely a protective device—only how did one break out of it? And how did one know when it was safe to emerge? Was she supposed to come out of her hole once a year and look for her shadow, like a groundhog?

She couldn't stand it if she allowed herself to become vulnerable, only to be crushed underfoot again.

The pâté was dreadful. The man had told her that pork liver would be just the thing, but it tasted awfully liverish. She wasn't hungry, anyway, and by nine o'clock she was in bed, if not asleep.

Actually she rather missed her Saturday night dates. Elliot hadn't been as exciting as . . . as Donovan, for instance, but he had been nice enough.

Her thoughts lingered stubbornly on the bulldozer operator. She had seen him around town several times, and he invariably awarded her one of his blindingly benevolent smiles. She had been torn between amusement and something slightly more uncomfortable once when she heard him calling the rotund, red-faced woman who worked at the fish market "little darlin'." He certainly tossed his legendary charm around indiscriminately! Not even to herself would Grace admit that she had rather enjoyed those casual endearments. Even "Pigtails" had had a certain warmth, and face it, warmth was a quality that was notably lacking in her present life.

Resolve stiffened. *Darned* if she'd allow herself to be taken in by another silver-tongued male! She had better things to do with her time—foremost of which was to get on with some drawings to go with the verses she had written. Lately she had been dreaming up the most incredible schmaltz! It had taken her a week to come up with an acceptable design for the verse about Love Blooming in the Garden of My Heart. She had finally hit on a scheme of red, heart-shaped anthurium blossoms for that one. Maybe she'd better stick to the breezier friendship cards for a while—the valentine award had gone to her head.

Saturday dawned with a promise of mildness. The sun was a flat gold disc in a field of pale turquoise, and Grace stared through the kitchen window at the tiny pink clouds that drifted up from Florida. As she sipped coffee she glanced through the bills, and it occurred to her that she had heard nothing from either Ogleby or Donovan about the ditching that had been done in her back yard to channel off rainwater. She dialed the rental agency and waited, idly twirling a white, beaded moccasin on one toe. The recorded voice crackled in her ear, telling her that at the sound of the tone . . .

She slammed down the phone. She'd write a letter rather than talk into that machine! She *hated* talking to a recorder! She ripped a page from her lined tablet and jotted a note to Mr. Ogleby to the effect that the work had been done and was satisfactory and as she hadn't heard from him, she assumed the owner had agreed to pay for the improvement. She signed her name, Grace B. Spencer, with a flourish, and readied it for mailing. There had been a time when she would have taken the absence of a bill as proof that she didn't owe anything, but not anymore. These days everything had to be spelled out.

The slight breeze that rustled through the reeds was a whispered enticement as Grace stood in the opened back door. Amazing how the ever-changing sea of reeds and rushes that bordered practically all of Georgia's coastline had become so dear to her. Perhaps in another life she had lived here beside the Golden Isles. She spread several crackers with the unfortunate liver pâté, grabbed her portfolio and locked the door behind her.

The southwest breeze brought a scent of creosote to mingle pleasantly with the sweet wax myrtles, the groundsel and the pungent salt-marsh smells. It had the usual tranquilizing effect. Grace breathed in deeply, gazing out across Back River and the marshes to Saint Simons Island. As far as she was concerned, you could keep the islands, with their reknown tourist facilities and famous golf courses. Due to an excess of orderliness in her youth, Grace preferred Brunswick's less restrictive atmosphere to the manicured charm of Jekyll, Sea Island, or even the larger Saint Simons. The liveoaks here were just as old, just as gracefully grotesque, the delightful old Victorian homes just as lovely as any of the opulent Victorian "cottages" in Millionaire's Village.

She'd far rather spend her time watching the colorful, hardworking shrimp boats come in than hang about the marinas, with their gleaming white sailboats and impeccable cruisers. She had even made friends with a few of the resident pelicans that waited for handouts from the seafood dealers on the Brunswick docks.

She sauntered along the narrow, winding road that separated the woods from the marshes and rounded the last curve before reaching her destination—and her jaw fell in stunned disbelief. She let fly an oath she had once heard a Marine sergeant use and glared at the line of red flags that led her affronted eye directly to the hatefully familiar blue truck. "QD!" she exclaimed, consigning the whole outfit to perdition. And then her mind connected the man, Donovan, with the words, and she swallowed convulsively and sank numbly to the ground. *QD. Quinn Donovan. Quinn Donovan Engineering.*

Had her father been right in his assessment of her mental acuity? She didn't rate alongside her two lawyer brothers, perhaps, but she had thought he was being grossly unfair when he had told her she couldn't think her way out of a paper bag. Still, why *should* she have suspected? One didn't ordinarily name an engineering firm after a bulldozer operator—or even a foreman.

"Oh, rats!" The ground was both colder and damper than she had expected, but eventually she rolled over onto her knees and took out her drawing pad. No point in even trying to write in this mood, and besides, she'd better get in all the sketching she could before the whole place was turned into a blasted resort community.

Half an hour passed and Grace was lost in the intricacies of design to be found in a few tendrils of Spanish moss. She wasn't at all sure how she could use it, but she drew, nevertheless, forcing her dismay undercover until she heard someone approaching through the dense underbrush.

Her chin jutted belligerently. She steeled herself to tell QD Engineering just what she thought of its despoiling a beautiful natural sanctuary, but when she felt something cold and wet nudge her back, she jumped and whirled around to confront a sleek brown dog. After an initial gasp Grace started to laugh, and the dog tilted its head inquiringly and then moved past her to nose into the paper bag of crackers and liver pâté.

"Be my guest," Grace offered and unwrapped the unappetizing lunch. She had thought that perhaps if she was really hungry, she'd eat the concoction. She had made mounds of it, and her thrifty nature deplored waste.

The dog devoured the works and whimpered softly for more. "Sorry, girl, that's it." The dog was probably only about half grown. She wore a collar and looked well kept, if a little thin, and Grace stroked the velvety head until the pup moved a few feet away, circled twice and curled up with her nose close to the torn paper bag.

It occurred to Grace that she might enjoy having a dog of some sort for companionship. The cats were nice, but the minute she allowed them in the house, they began playing with her plants, swatting the leaves to ribbons, tumbling pots and using the dirt for other purposes. A dog might be just what she needed.

Musing on the possibility, she turned back onto her knees and elbows and studied a flat rosette of curly leaves she found growing under the cover of the tall dried grass. She had peeled off her sweater, and now she could feel the sun beating down on the black cotton turtleneck shirt. She could also feel the cool air on the strip of bare flesh where the shirt had parted company with her jeans, but she was almost finished. Peering

closer to see the way the tiny leaves curled tightly into
the center of the rosette, she was oblivious to the soft
natural sounds around her. From the corner of her eye
she saw the pup get up and, sensing her approach, she
waved a hand absently behind her. "Just a minute, girl.
I've almost got it."

The voice that answered her was definitely not
canine, nor was it female. "I don't know about the view
from where you are, honey, but from here it's spectacular."

She twisted around on her knees as the voice
slammed with stunning force into her midsection. For a
man who must weigh over two hundred pounds, Quinn
Donovan had no business being so light on his feet!
"Do you make a habit of sneaking up and spying on
people? And why didn't you tell me who you were!
And what do you think you're going to do with this
land? There are agencies to protect lands like this, you
know—Tidal Wetlands Protection, Coastal Manage-
ment and the wildlife people, to name a few!"

Before she realized his intention, Donovan had
levered himself onto the ground beside her and picked
up her drawing pad. She snatched it from his hands and
suffered a look of mild surprise instead of his usual
ready grin.

He retorted, "Do you make a habit of kidnapping a
man's dog and holding her captive when he's doing his
best to train her? Are you planning on drawing those
creesey greens, or cooking them, and since when did
you become eligible to claim squatter's rights on this
particular tract of land?"

The small, pink clouds of the morning had turned
into a gray, amorphous mass that now blotted out the
sun, reminding Grace that it was midwinter, not Indian
summer. She tugged unobtrusively at her shirt and shot
a rueful look in Quinn's direction. "Sorry. I got carried

away. Sometimes I'm a little less than ept, socially." At least she was where overpowering men with stunning smiles were concerned. "Is this your dog?"

"Meet Mollie Brown, better known for her appetite than for her intellect."

"What is she?"

"Drop. Cross between a pointer and a setter. Supposed to make a good bird dog, but this one's not going to put much meat on the table."

Grace suppressed a shudder, but Quinn didn't miss her look of distaste. "Is it a matter of principle, or are you a vegetarian?" He lifted one of those wicked eyebrows and she stared at him, completely losing the train of conversation. The magnetic field around the man was unbelievable! If he should come within ten feet of her on a pitch-black night, she'd know it. She'd *feel* it in the very marrow of her bones!

"Neither, actually," she managed when she could trust her voice again. "I like meat as well as the next person, and I don't go in for plastic shoes, either, but I can't bear the thought of troops of ruthless hunters charging through the fields armed to the teeth, with—"

He picked up on the theme. "With slavering hounds baying and snapping at the heels of the helpless quarry." Shaking his head gently, he said, "Sweet child, have you any idea what happens to the game population when men start taking over their territory for highways and homes? Hunters are as interested in wildlife survival as you are. At least hunting thins 'em out so that those that survive have the vitality to breed. X number of acres will support X number of animals. It's as simple as that—and as complex." His hand moved to her drawing pad again, but she intercepted his reach and tucked the pad into her portfolio.

"And hunters are the world's best at rationalizing," she said flatly.

"Aren't we all when it comes to what we want?" he admitted with a twist of his usual smile. "But Mollie happens to be the only hound I own at the moment, so you can rest easy—ol' Moll's not going to disturb the game population to any great extent."

Some of the inexplicable tension drained from Grace's slender body as she sat, knees drawn up before her, three feet away from the large man. "At least not when there are crackers spread with liver pâté to lure her away from the trail," she agreed with a reluctant smile.

"Mollie, you old scoundrel, have you been moochin' again?" He tugged the dog's ears affectionately and shook his head in mock despair. "My neighbors can't have a barbecue anymore without telling me ahead of time so I can lock this thieving hound up. You wouldn't believe the number of T-bones that have turned up on my front stoop. Not the steaks, mind you—just the bones."

Grace laughed and felt the last of her tension go as Quinn's insidious friendliness began to work on her defenses. When he told her that he had a standing policy of feeding all of Mollie's victims, she was shamefully easy to persuade. She assured herself that it was only due to the fact that her stomach was beginning to protest the skipped meal. Besides, her social life had come to a standstill since Elliot had defected.

"Thanks, but it's really not necessary." Pride made one last stand.

"Nonsense. Gives me a perfect opportunity to show off my hand with Brunswick Stew."

It was embarrassingly easy to allow herself to be persuaded. She had tried to make the famous Georgia stew herself, and her efforts had not been notably successful. Perhaps she could pick up a few pointers. *Now who's rationalizing,* she jeered silently.

They hiked along the winding trail to the truck, and Quinn told her that the red flags were only staking out a hidden creek. "This ridge drops down into the marsh just past that stand of trees. Makes it dicey, what with all the wetland restrictions. We're studying the feasibility of draining this piece, but whatever we do, it will have the least possible impact on the ecology," he assured her. One more indication that Quinn Donovan was something more than just a bulldozer operator.

Grace closed her mind to the impact any development would have on her own beloved domain. She had always known it had to end sometime, with the growing popularity of the area and the spectacular view. Besides, what good would it do to protest to Donovan? He was only following orders from the property owner.

What am I doing here? she asked herself a dozen times on the drive to Donovan's home. For an encore I might try putting my head in a lion's mouth!

At the first glimpse of Quinn's house her preconceptions of the man shifted at once again. They turned off a narrow blacktop onto a shelled driveway that wound through tall, straight pines and enormous liveoaks, dripping with graybeards of moss. The house, a modest-sized rectangle painted a shade between pewter and olive, faced a bend of the river and a stunning view of marshes, from which loomed several stark skeletons of ancient cypress trees, bleached white by sun and salt air. There were signs of another, larger building, still in the early stages, connected to the smaller one by a broad, open-sided corridor. Both the site and the partially finished house bespoke a surprisingly cultivated taste, as well as the means to support it.

Inside Quinn invited her to make herself at home and strode through into what she supposed was a kitchen. For several moments Grace stood where she was, gazing around the long, driftwood-paneled room.

There were two skylights and a sliding glass door that opened onto the connecting corridor, but other than that, the only window in sight was a fan-shaped stained glass one in the gable end of the rectangular room.

"If you want to wash up, it's the other door," he called out.

No mistaking the door he meant. There were only two of them, other than the glass one. The large, open space seemed to combine living, sleeping and dining facilities, using a minimum of furnishings. Very spartan, she mused, but very effective.

Grace crossed the dark, softly gleaming pine floor and found herself in a compact bathroom that boasted putty-colored furnishings and a peeled cedar tree running from floor to ceiling, the branches of which had been trimmed back to make a towel rack. A sweat-stained khaki shirt hung from one stub and without thinking, she reached out and touched it.

Hurriedly she splashed her hands and face and left the intimate room for the more impersonal atmosphere of the larger one. From the kitchen she could hear reassuring noises, and she sniffed in appreciation of the enticing aroma that was beginning to drift out.

"Won't be long now," Quinn called out. "I had to pen Mollie up to keep her from climbing onto the stove. That pup's pure appetite!" He emerged with a handful of silver to find her studying one of the several paintings on the rough, gray-green paneled walls. "Like it?"

Grace frowned thoughtfully. "I'm not sure. I'd be willing to bet it was done by a man, though."

"You'd win. Edward, my youngest brother. These were some of his earlier works, before he started making all the juried shows. I can't afford him now."

The conversation followed easily from her question

about his other brothers and sisters, and she discovered that Quinn was the oldest of seven. He told her readily enough that all but Edward were married and caught up with families, careers or both.

"What about you?" she ventured over the ambrosial Brunswick Stew that had been served hot from the oven with a crown of puff pastry over the deep rame-kins.

"Your turn," he evaded skillfully. "Sisters, brothers, parents? What brought you down to the land of peaches and sunshine?"

"Surely you jest." The sky outside had turned leaden and with the blotting out of the sun had come a damp, penetrating cold.

"We throw in an occasional day like this just to remind you of what you left behind when you came south," he teased. "Seriously, Grace, how did you find your way to Georgia?" She had traded him her first name for the promise to forget her pigtail.

"I came for my great-aunt's funeral and stayed on to look after Uncle Henry. When he died, I was well settled in, with a temporary job in hand and the promise of a full-time teaching position at MCV. Besides, if I left, who'd look after the cats and the houseplants?" He had commented on the number of pets he had seen draped around the various porches the day he had come to do the ditching. "Which reminds me, Quinn—what exactly do you have to do with QD Engineering, and what are you doing playing around on top of that overgrown matchbox toy, and how come you're doing odd jobs for Ogleby?" She paused to catch her breath. "I can't figure you out at all."

"Did you ever consider a job with Gallup or Elmo Roper? No. On second thought, pollsters are obliged to stop asking questions long enough to listen for an-swers." He grinned across the satin surface of a sturdy walnut table, and Grace heard a yellow alert sounding in the recesses of her brain. He refilled her glass from the carafe of rosé and said, "No more about me. If we're going to be friends, we have to keep this thing balanced out, and so far all I know about you is that you teach art at a junior college, you've a soft spot for animals and you've got a mind like a zigzag sewing machine."

Grace reached for her glass—she really shouldn't; she wasn't used to more than a single glass of white wine with her dinner—as often as not to disguise one of her spectacular culinary failures. "What do you mean —about my mind, that is, and what gave you the idea I teach art? And the cats aren't really mine, you know. They just live there, the same as I do."

"There, you see what I mean? Zigzag. Three subjects in one breath."

The wine sent a glow of warmth stealing up over her face. How could she have been so wrong about the man? He was remarkably good company. "I merely answered the three questions you asked—in one breath."

Quinn laughed and reached out a long forefinger to touch the tip of her nose. It burned like fire. "You have an impertinent nose, Grace Spencer. With your dreamer's eyes, it makes an intriguing combination. Did you honestly think you could disguise them by dressing like a prison matron and screwing your hair up into a hard knot?"

She backed away from his hand. It fell to her shoulder and lingered there, as if he had forgotten to withdraw it, and suddenly the wine rushed to her head and she pushed aside her chair and stood, dismayed to find that she was not altogether steady on her feet. "I'm not used to drinking in the middle of the day." She sounded breathless, and it didn't help to see the amused indulgence with which Quinn was regarding her.

"Relax, honey. I'm not planning to ply you with Brunswick Stew and then, when you're off guard, pounce on you," he rumbled softly.

Moving with unaccustomed awkwardness to stare at another of the stark, nonobjective paintings on the wall, she said, "I didn't think you were." It was the wine—it *must* have been the wine—that made her add, "You told me the first time we met that I wasn't your type."

He was behind her, almost touching her, having moved with that unexpected agility that seemed so out of place in a man his size. "Little girls with pigtails," he murmured in amused recollection. "I almost didn't recognize you when I saw you all dressed up in that cast-iron outfit you wear to school, with your hair all nailed to your head."

There was no room for either indignation or amusement. He was too close, his breath creating treacherous currents on her nape. She stared in desperate concentration at the acrylic painting until she felt his hands come down on her shoulders, and then she sagged in defeat. The few inches between them disappeared, and she let her head fall back onto his shoulder. A pushover. That's what she was. After all her fine resolutions, the first shot fired and she went up in a puff of smoke.

His hands cupped her shoulders, warming her, disarming her, and when she felt his lips against her temple, the unfamiliar brush of his mustache against the throbbing pulse there, her eyes closed in defeat. It had been so long . . .

"Grace," he whispered, and the rough sound tumbled down her spinal column like dominoes to jar dormant nerves into life again.

He turned her and she was ready for him, her face lifted and her lips tremulous with need. "Grace," he whispered again, just before she felt the soft brush of his mustache and then the shattering touch of his mouth. It was a devastating act of possession. It was as if a charge of electricity had been building up between them until it could no longer be contained. In the explosion she was aware of a hundred blinding sensations at once; of the firmness of his lips in contrast to the tantalizing texture of his mustache, the taste of him and the scent of him—masculine, clean, outdoorsy. Her hands moved, one to the side of his neck, the other to the thick, black curls. Their vitality was overwhelming, as was his. The solid warmth of his hard body was impressed on her every cell, like coming home, as his arms tightened to weld her even closer. One hand dropped to the seat of her jeans, tucking familiarly under the curve of her hips to bring her into stunning proximity to his potent masculinity.

When his lips lifted so that he could ensnare her with his warm, dark gaze, she managed to maneuver one hand between them and push. "Don't be frightened," he murmured, and she shook her head frantically.

"No—I mean, I'm not frightened, only—no, please, Quinn." She was hardly coherent, but he seemed to understand and his grip on her eased, allowing her to back away a single step. This she did, drawing a shaky breath and fixing her gaze on the painting just beyond him. *Think,* Grace Spencer! For once in your life, *think* first! There's only one inevitable end to a beginning like this and that's in his bed. You'll end up being made a fool of again! Her mind raced madly, gathering up every argument it could find and slamming them out like a computer printout. This man devours women with about as much thought as he'd give a bowl of corn flakes, and if at his age he hasn't settled down, then he's not the settling kind. Do you want to risk going through all that again?

"I think I'd better get out of here," she blurted.

The slow smile spread over his face, but it was as if she were seeing it from behind a dark glass wall. His hands ran down from her shoulders to her hands and then he put her away from him. "You still haven't told me the story of your life," he reminded her, but some of the warmth was missing, as if he were already losing interest in her.

"You'd be bored stiff." She managed to inject a note of disinterest in her voice as she moved across to where she had dropped her sweater and her portfolio. "I hate to have to ask for a lift home, but this is out of my territory."

"No problem. I've got an appointment in town later on, anyway. Can you spare me a minute to change clothes and stash these things away?" He gestured toward the table and Grace put down her things again.

"Better yet, I'll clear away while you change." She preferred to even the score between them, if possible. No loose ends to ensnare her later on.

She heard the sound of the shower as she was loading the dishwasher, and ten minutes later Quinn appeared in the door, dressed in gray flannels and a red knit shirt. His hair glistened with dampness as he glanced appreciatively around the neat kitchen. "Woman's deft touch. Makes a man realize what he's been missing." There was an edge of sarcasm to his voice, but when Grace glared at him, an accusation of sexism on her lips, she saw nothing but a suspiciously bland smile and she subsided uneasily.

She reached for her sweater and pulled it on over her head. "I'm ready when you are," she told him, tugging her sweater down around her hips. This unpredictable man had a disconcerting way of throwing her off balance, and the sooner she got away, the better. One hand lifted defensively to her hair. Then, tilting her chin, she reminded herself that it didn't make the slightest bit of difference how she looked, because Quinn Donovan meant less than nothing to her. This had been an interesting interlude, but it wouldn't be repeated.

Her determination was reinforced when he led her past the blue truck to a low, powerful looking sports car, the kind one might expect a swinging bachelor to drive. There was certainly no room in her well-ordered future for any swinging bachelors, and according to the gossip this one swung in a wider orbit than most. He'd hardly have any interest in a not-so-young schoolteacher, except perhaps as a passing curiosity.

Not until he pulled up in front of her house and cut the engine did it occur to Grace that she still didn't know any more about Quinn Donovan than the fact that he was one of seven children, and that was hardly relevant. He came around and opened the door for her. Always the perfect gentleman, she sneered silently, forcing a degree of rancor into her traitorous thoughts.

Adopting her most effective schoolmarm tone, she said, "Thank you for the meal, Quinn. I won't ask you in, since you have an appointment."

He nodded perfunctorily. His usual smile was noticeably absent, and there was a look about his shuttered eyes that Grace interpreted as ennui. "Hope it makes up for the pâté Mollie swiped. See you around."

She let herself in the front door as the long, low sports car snarled away, conscious of a feeling of anticlimax. It was almost six, too late for a regular business appointment, and anyway, who kept business appointments on a Saturday evening? He was probably headed to see his hard-edged lady friend. One of them, at least. Men like Quinn Donovan didn't sit at home on a Saturday night with a good book. Or even a bad one.

Disconsolately Grace dropped her portfolio and went through to the kitchen. She poured milk into a bowl and frowned at the covered plastic dish of pâté. "Rats," she growled and took them both out to the side porch where her family of cats waited. Abstractedly watching them crouch around the two containers, she allowed her troubled thoughts to rise to the surface of her mind. Evidently she was not as secure as she had thought, in more than one respect. How long ago had she been counting her blessings? A career, a home and Elliot. One down, two to go, and that was only the least of her worries.

The feelings that were beginning to assail her now bore no resemblance to those she had felt for Don so long ago. She had been a girl then—heedless, impressionable and terribly vulnerable. Now she was a woman —heedless, impressionable and, she feared, more vulnerable than ever.

Chapter Five

"Grace, dear, if you'd only told us, I'm sure we could have made other arrangements," her mother apologized, and Grace murmured something to the effect that it wasn't important, that she had several options for the holidays. Mendaciously she mentioned the possibility of staying at one of the better-known resort hotels over on Jekyll, and her mother latched on to the mutual face-saver with obvious relief. "Oh, aren't you the lucky one? While we're up here shivering under blankets of snow and ice, you'll be basking on a beach somewhere getting a lovely suntan. Why don't you invite Jill to join you? The poor child deserves a nice vacation, I'm sure." Mother had never been particularly interested in her daughters.

After a morning's deliberation Grace did just that. Not even to herself would she admit to being hurt by her parents' lack of welcome—other guests, the boys and their families, not enough bedrooms to go around, were pretty weak excuses to her way of thinking. A militant sparkle in her eyes, she dialed her sister's number.

Jill was cross, having been roused from her bed, but she soon warmed to the idea of a vacation on Jekyll Island. "I don't know if I can afford to fly, though, Gracey, and I *can't* go by train. It would take forever, and you know how long, tedious trips always make me look like a hag."

It was decided that Grace would pay for a round-trip airline ticket, but in the end Grace hung up with a feeling of satisfaction. At least *one* member of her family cared enough to want to spend the holidays with her. Of course, Jill would have to understand that there wouldn't be any extra package under the tree for her come Christmas morning. It was going to take all her prize money and most of her savings to finance this impulsive gesture, not that she regretted it for one minute.

She phoned three of the beach hotels before she found one with an available double and managed to stifle her gasp when she was told the cost of three days. Before she could unclamp her fingers from the phone, someone banged peremptorily on the door and she shook off her dismay and hurried through to answer the summons.

"What are you doing here?"

Quinn braced himself against the brash green clapboard siding and beamed at her. "Good morning to you, too, honey. What happened? Cat got your tongue?"

Feeling her spurious poise begin to crumble inside her, she glowered up at him silently.

"Only one question?" he marveled gently. "Practically speechless with pleasure at the sight of me, aren't you?" He reached for the screened door, and she held the latch from inside.

It had been over a week since she had seen him, and the spell of his potent masculine magnetism had begun to face. It returned full force now, washing over her like the legendary seventh wave, and she came up sputtering. "Not particularly! If you—I don't—what do you want?" she blurted, and then she stood back helplessly as he opened the screen and came inside, closing both doors after him.

His eyes strayed around the unused front room, cluttered with old-fashioned furniture, china knick-knacks and those of her plants that preferred a northern exposure. She had moved most of the old furniture in here when she began to acquire a few things of her own. He picked up a small bisque shepherdess, and Grace was struck by the contrast of the delicate china ornament and the sinewy, tanned hand, the back of which was liberally laced with black hairs. "You can tell a lot about a person by the things they collect," he mused.

Wrapping her arms around her in an unconsciously defensive gesture, Grace said coolly, "These aren't my things. At least, they are now, but I didn't—they belonged to my great-aunt and -uncle."

"Still, you elected to keep them, so I guess they're a part of your home environment, along with the jungle"—he gestured to the shelves full of houseplants—"and that shameless bunch of freeloaders. Your cats," he elucidated at her puzzled look.

If Grace was to be judged, she preferred it to be by her own possessions—the attractive modern rug she had assembled from mill samples, the two or three good serigraphs she had bought and the yellow linen slipcovered sofa she had been lucky enough to find at a secondhand store. "What do you want?" she blurted, sounding ungracious, if not actually rude. He affected her that way. It was all she could do not to run and dive under the bed until he was gone! "And stop grinning at me!" she exclaimed angrily. "You—you make me nervous!"

"Do I, little one? Do I, indeed? Invite me into your parlor for a cup of coffee and maybe I'll tell you what I want." He was still grinning—fatuously, Grace decided, and she blew impatiently at a strand of hair as she moved aside and gestured to the French doors.

The astounding nerve of the man, she bristled five minutes later. He invited himself in for coffee and then had the nerve to criticize just because she had left the morning's brew on the woodstove to stay warm! She plunked her mug down with no consideration for its fragility and glared at him. His tautly muscled body in the beige corduroy jeans and black knit shirt was perfectly relaxed on her sofa. He had talked with infuriating blandness about the weather, the economic impact of the closing of a large local plant and the recent decline in the shrimp harvest. Eyeing his half-empty mug meaningfully, Grace waited for him to come to the point of his visit.

"When do you break for the holidays?" he asked, and she told him she'd be free as of Thursday. He continued, "You're going home to the frozen North?"

"No."

He waited, looking every bit as much at ease as the battered tomcat who called her porch home, and as the silence expanded she was drawn unwillingly into elaborating. "My sister's coming. We're going to spend the holidays at Jekyll." When he lifted one of those darkly mocking eyebrows, she felt a surge of satisfaction. If she had occasionally felt twinges of self-pity because of the rift with her own family, this made up for it. How many people would leap at a chance to stay at a plush resort on one of the Golden Isles? The fact that she was not one of them was beside the point. Donovan didn't know that.

"I was going to invite you to spend Christmas with me," he said to her utter astonishment.

"Why on earth would you do that?"

He shrugged. "Now that you mention it, I don't really know. Guess it just occurred to me that you might enjoy it."

As she stared at him in amazement a dull flush rose over his hard-hewn features, and once more Grace found herself scrambling madly to regain her balance at the erratic swing of her own weathervane emotions. Just when she thought she had him figured out . . . !

"Well, thank you, Quinn, but of course, it's out of the question, even if Jill weren't coming." Darn! She sounded so prim—so mealymouthed! To cover her confusion, she stood and reached abruptly for his mug. One of his hands closed around her wrist like a warm, solicitous manacle, and she tugged impatiently. "Quinn, don't be childish!"

But there was nothing at all childish about the touch of his gentle but iron-hard hand, about the sight of those tanned, powerful fingers circling her delicate wrist. She strained every muscle in an attempt to pull away, but it was no use. The sound of his laughter registered a seven on her internal seismograph, and he tugged her off balance so that she fell into his lap. And then his mouth came down to shut off her indignant protest.

System after system closed down in her mind until only sensation remained—drinking in the taste, the smell and the feel of him. He shifted her so that she was half under him, and his weight pressed the breath from her lungs. She gloried in it, gloried in the swiftly mounting tension of his body that told her of her effect on him.

And even that was hardly greater than his effect on *her!* Reaching up to push him away, she felt the muscular swell of his pectorals, heard the swift intake of his breath, and then his mouth sought her own again, edging her toward insanity with its predatory explorations.

His hand was sliding downward along her thigh, raking her button-front skirt along with it, and she hadn't even noticed when it had come undone. Frantically she caught at his fingers. "Quinn, don't—you can't do that!'"

The hand moved obediently upward. She felt the heat of his palm on her bare flesh as it slid over her stomach and then began to move inexorably downward once more. Inside her something fluttered fiercely and then coalesced into a hard, hot aching that left her moaning under her breath. "Quinn, Quinn, please."

"Yes, Grace," he sighed softly.

That wasn't what she meant! His hand moved to her breast, stroking the coral-tipped cone into proud sentience, and she wondered bewilderedly when he had undone her bra—or had she? This was insane! She writhed beneath him, struggling against the honeyed sweetness of her own inertia to escape the tender prison of his arms, his powerful legs. He laughed down at her. The gleam of satisfaction—or was it triumph?—in his eyes was all but hidden under the dense thicket of his lashes.

"You're right, Grace—this couch wasn't meant for two." Before she could grasp his meaning, he stood and lifted her in his arms, turning toward the open door of her bedroom.

No, no, no! The words screamed silently in her mind, but she lacked the strength to voice them, lacked the will to deny herself the wildly fulfilling pleasures he promised her. Her shirt had fallen open, and the shred of white lace that was her bra hung from her shoulders like a scarf. Quinn's eyes roamed hungrily over her bared breasts, taking pride in the obvious state of her arousal before lowering her tenderly onto the bed.

The moment his hand went to his belt she stiffened *Was* this what she wanted?

Want didn't enter into it! She *wanted* him like a starving man wants food! Her eyes clung hungrily to the narrow-hipped, broad-shouldered figure that threatened the low ceiling of her room. His shirt fell away, and her eyes clung in fascination to the small red-brown accents of male nipples that nestled in the curling pelt on his chest. His body hair was sooty black, curling in tight, flat ringlets. And then her gaze lifted unwillingly to his face, past the thrust of his squared jaw, past the sensuous mouth that was barely smiling now, the aggressive mustache. It darted back to that smile again before lifting to his eyes. A chilly doubt crept into her overheated consciousness, like the small drafts that found their way through the very walls of the creaky old house.

Was she wrong? No. There was an element of self-satisfaction, of . . . of *conspiracy* in that smile she had never noticed before, almost as if they shared an amusing secret.

"Quinn?" she whispered uncertainly, and he came down beside her, his body naked except for the trim navy blue briefs, and she scrambled away. He was magnificent. He was the quintessential male animal, and it was that very quality that pierced through her like a shard of ice. He reached for her, but she escaped to the other side of the wide brass bed, her wary eyes never once leaving his face.

"What is it, Grace?" Some of the sureness seeped from his ebony eyes, leaving a look of irritation in its place. "A little late to be having second thoughts, isn't it?"

"First thoughts, Quinn. What happened had nothing to do with *thought,* and you know it." She was standing beside the bed, her shirt wrapped around her as she stared accusingly down at his large, reclining form.

"It's a little late to be changing your mind, darlin'," he mocked, and anger ignited inside her, racing through her until she was trembling with it.

"Changing my mind! You're absolutely insane! I politely reached for your cup and you grabbed me! And after barging in here uninvited in the first place!"

"Oh, honey, I was invited," he said, his voice softly ominous. "I'm a little too old to be playing games, but if that's the way you want it, then I guess I can go along with it."

"Playing games! I think your macho reputation has gone to your head!" Her fingers worked frantically to close the buttons of her skirt, but there was no way she could get herself hooked back into her bra with any semblance of dignity and she gave up and fastened her blouse with fumbling haste. "Just because a—a bunch of schoolgirls think you're—you're—just don't make the mistake of believing every woman you meet is going to fall for all that—"

"All right, honey, I get the message—the real message, this time." Nonchalantly he proceeded to dress, and there was nothing she could do but stand there and wait, because he blocked her passage to the door. That hateful grin mocked her inability to turn away. "As a matter of academic curiosity, Miss Spencer, just what did you think you were inviting? Did you expect me to watch the sunset over Sidney's marsh and swap sugary little verses with you? Or maybe you thought we'd carve our initials in the Lover's Oak." The hard glitter of his eyes never left her while he stretched to ram his shirttail into his pants.

Grace could feel the color drain from her face. Quinn's gaze narrowed, and she knew with hateful certainty just what he was thinking. "Don't worry," she jeered, "I'm not about to swoon! Even if I were the vaporish sort, it would take a lot more than an over-grown, underbred, asinine, self-appointed Romeo like you to make me faint! You know what you can do with your corn-fed Lothario act? I'll tell you what—"

"Honey, did anyone ever tell you you have a tongue like a double-edged saw? I'm afraid you've been on the shelf a little too long for my taste, so if you've had your thrill-of-the-month, I'll be shoving off. Oh, and by the way—after the first of the year, you'd better start looking around for another place to stay. I'm thinking of tearing down this house as soon after the holidays as I can get around to it."

Before she could summon her wits to reply, he was gone, closing each door behind him with exquisite control.

On Thursday morning Grace talked with the school administrator. The source of the complaint was not named, but she had little doubt that it was Celia Putney, the librarian. She promised to do something about her disorderly morning classes and was remind-ed, not for the first time, that MCV was a serious career center and hers was the only class about which there had been complaints.

Hardly surprising. Elliot had problems with disci-pline, too, but Celia would hardly complain about the noise coming from Business Math 1A, even if they took to playing "Chopsticks" on their calculators! She had seen him stopping by the library several times a day lately. Maybe now that the smug little blonde librarian had finally snared her man, Grace would be left to handle her discipline problem in peace.

Jill's flight, a pieced-together arrangement that had been the best Grace could do at short notice, came into McKinnon, over on Saint Simons. The drive back across the Torras Causeway was filled with Jill's chatter about the man who had sat next to her from Atlanta. Grace listened for a while and then her thoughts veered off in a totally unwelcome direction, as they had been doing all too often lately.

It had been three days since Quinn had burst in on her with his preposterous behavior, three days in which she had examined her own responses for a clue as to what had made him react the way he had. As if *she* had made overtures to *him*, for goodness' sake! Surely he didn't think that just because she took him up on his invitation to lunch that day—?

Impossible! No man could be that dense. Still, Donovan was used to having every woman who came in range of his bone-melting smile fall down in mute adoration. Perhaps he took her for just another gullible, sex-starved female—and unfortunately she wasn't in any position yet to deny it. Her own resistance was an iffy proposition, but she was working on it.

That parting crack, about finding herself another place to stay, had almost been overlooked while she had curled up in a withdrawn huddle on the couch and brought herself down to a slow simmer. She had dialed Ogleby and got his answering service, then shelved the problem until after the holidays.

"—and so I told him that I wasn't about to play house, even if it was aboard a sixty-foot yacht, and he said—" Jill's rather high-pitched voice drifted in and out of Grace's awareness as she slowed up for the toll gate—the parking fee, it was called—on Jekyll Island.

Fortunately Jill did not seem to notice Grace's inattention. She expressed delight at the luxurious accommodations and preened for a small group of male golfers on their way to the links while Grace got them registered. The weather had decided to cooperate, fortunately, and Jill immediately sought the sheltered area of the pool, where she arranged herself in a stunning pose and waited for further developments.

Grace curled up under the shade of a large beach umbrella with her writing pad and pen and stared absently out across the flawless grounds to a strip of blue Atlantic, casting an occasional indulgent smile across to where Jill reigned. She had forgotten how giddy her baby sister was—and how absolutely adorable. For all her innocent self-centeredness, there wasn't a malicious bone in her stunning little body.

Donovan—any man at all—could be excused for mistaking one of Jill's seductive little smiles for a come-on, but how anyone could think that Grace—! With a snort of disgust she shook Donovan from her thoughts.

With no one to feed her cats, Grace found it necessary to make a trip home each day, a matter of twenty minutes or so each way. The day after Christmas she left the hotel just before lunchtime, having satisfied herself that Jill was being entertained. Jill had struck up a friendship with an unattached girl about her own age, Julee Something-or-other, and the two of them seemed bent on reeling in every available male in sight and some, Grace feared, who were not all that available.

It was a relief to let herself into her comfortably

shabby living room. The cats twined about her ankles, and she lifted the tomcat and tickled him under his wide, scarred head. After feeding them and checking the plants and the mailbox, she dialed Ogleby's office again. If he was planning to demolish her home out from under her, the least he could do was to find her something else she could afford. She closed her mind to the pain of knowing that her own private sanctuary would soon be someone's housing development.

Five minutes later she dropped the phone into its cradle and stared numbly at the water stain above the chimney. Quinn Donovan again. Was there no escaping the man? Ogleby had informed her that he knew of no plans for the immediate razing of the house, but he'd check with the owner, Mr. Donovan, and let her know. Grace had not even had to ask which Mr. Donovan. When she was able to regain her wits, she came up with the answer to one of the questions that had been keeping her awake for the past few nights.

No wonder Quinn Donovan had acted as if he owned her! He was just the sort of conceited chauvinist who'd expect to exercise the old *droit du seigneur*. Grace had known all along that she was paying a shamefully low rate, but it was the same figure Uncle Henry had paid. After he had died, Grace had just continued to mail in the check by the first of each month, and nothing had ever been said about bringing it up to today's level. On her side nothing had ever been said about bringing the house up to acceptable standards, either, until the bathroom problem had gotten out of hand.

Ogleby promised to see what he could do to find her something else. Even if Quinn had just been bluffing when he threatened to bring the place down around her ears—or words to that effect—she couldn't go on living there now that she knew who her real landlord was.

This business had all the earmarks of another sticky situation involving her with a man and his property, and she refused to let it happen. She had a good life going for herself and she wasn't about to jeopardize it now. Quinn Donovan could play his little games with some other hapless victim—she was just a little too smart to get caught in the same trap twice!

The day before Jill was to return to New York, Grace drove her around Brunswick, showing her several of the town's attractions. She pointed out that the town had been laid out in 1771, with the streets and parks named by the Colonial Council of the Royal Province of Georgia. Jill wrinkled her nose and commented on the pervasive odor from the pulp and paper mill. They drove past Lanier's Oak, and Grace told her about Georgia's most famous poet and his best known work, the *Marshes of Glynn*, written about the marshes off Brunswick. *"Beautiful glooms, soft dusks in the noon-day fire/Wildwood privacies, closets of lone desire,"* she quoted the Sidney Lanier poem, and Jill gazed at her with puzzlement in her lovely, lavender-blue eyes. "I don't get it, but it's pretty. I like poems that rhyme." Grace decided to show her MCV and then call it quits.

On the way she pointed out Lover's Oak, a nine-hundred-year-old liveoak at the corner of Prince and Albany streets, considered passing on the legend of the Indian maiden and her lover and sighed. She suddenly felt so tired—so awfully much older than her beautiful younger sister.

"So—here's where I do my dastardly deeds," she quipped lightly, pulling up in front of the ugly red-brick administration building. Another car pulled up in the circular drive behind her, and while they sat there, Elliot strode past, cast an embarrassed glance at Grace's car and then did a double-take. She smiled sympathetically. Elliot had been comical in his attempts to avoid her since that night at the supper club, when Donovan had hinted at an intimacy that didn't exist—then.

"Jill, this is Elliot Rand, MCV's star math instructor. Elliot, my sister, Jill, and if she looks familiar to you, it's because she's one of New York's fastest rising models." She was amused to note that Jill, offering her truly stunning smile, did not bother to deny the plaudit. Elliot preened visibly, cleared his throat and offered to show Jill around the school.

"Oh, great! Come on, Grace." Jill couldn't help responding to any halfway attractive male, and Elliot was no exception. She had no idea of the constraint between Grace and the math teacher, but Grace took pity on Elliot's sensibilities and begged off.

"If you don't mind, I'll just wait here. I see enough of that place during term."

A little stiffly Elliot informed her that he'd be delighted to see Miss Spencer home if Grace preferred not to wait.

Watching the pair of them stroll up the front walk, Elliot's stocky form bent solicitously over Jill's golden mop of curls, it occurred to her that they were really an extremely handsome pair—and oddly alike in some ways. Then, with an inexplicable desire to cry, she pulled away from the curb and headed home. A block away, waiting at the stop light, she saw Quinn's sports car pull out of her driveway and head away from town.

Well, drat the man! Her vision blurred as the quick tears rose to the surface. No doubt he'd been checking to see if she'd vacated the premises yet! She was paid up through the next five days and had no intention of getting out one hour before she had to!

A ludicrous image of herself standing guard against a threatening bulldozer popped into her mind, and she bit her lip on a tremulous smile. Heavens, talk about an emotional mess! She had a bad case of fantods! The honking of horns behind her alerted her to the fact that the light had turned green again.

Chapter Six

On the last day of the year Ogleby called to tell her that Quinn Donovan had decreed she could stay where she was for the time being. And if she wanted to change, anyway, the least expensive thing he could offer her as an alternative was almost twice what she was currently paying and was six miles away from MCV.

"Rats!" So much for her heroic stand! She was almost disappointed that she couldn't take a self-righteous attitude and move out, but she had to be practical. With Jill's airline ticket and the cost of their brief plunge into the lap of luxury, she could ill afford that sort of gesture. What she'd better be concerning herself with was hanging on to her job and getting a batch of work off to Mr. Harris. The checks took an unconscionable amount of time coming through even after he'd accepted her things, although with interest rates the way they were, she couldn't blame him for wanting to squeeze every last drop out of a dollar before passing it on.

There was always a letdown after the holidays. This year it seemed abysmal. Perhaps it was because she was a year older. On the bright side February was not far off, and The Valentine would be hitting the market any day now. She had the supply Mr. Harris had sent her as soon as it was printed, but seeing it for sale in the stores was an altogether different thrill. No matter how many times it happened, she still found herself inventing excuses to go into the places that sold the All Seasons line, lingering around the display in hopes she'd see someone actually select one of her designs. So far it hadn't happened, but *someone* was buying the things. Mr. Harris reported that her sales were slowly increasing, especially in the Southeast.

The second day back at school Donovan waylaid her before she could get across the parking lot. She saw him ease out of his truck as she strode briskly toward the Florence Fowler Building, where her classes were held, and did her best to ignore him until he swung into step beside her.

"Morning, Grace."

Casting an irritated glance from the corner of her eye, she was astounded to see the familiar broad grin on his face, just as if he had never tried to seduce her and then insulted her when his best efforts failed! He caught at her arm and she jerked it out of his grasp, spinning around to glare at him. "Look, Donovan, if you have anything to say to me, then say it through Ogleby!"

Dark, wings-of-the-devil eyebrows lifted in mild reproof. "You do go in for the indirect approach, don't you, darlin'? As it happens, though, what I wanted to see you about has nothing to do with our relationship."

"We don't *have* a relationship, Donovan!" She

stalked off, every tendon in her long, graceful neck in evidence as she thrust her chin forward.

He was beside her before she had gone two steps. "Sure we do, honey—landlord and tenant, to name one."

"To name the *only* one!"

"Still insist on playing games, hmmm?" They came to an opening in the low brick wall that surrounded the parking lot, and he blocked her way. Short of scrambling in an undignified manner over the three-foot barrier, there was nothing she could do but hear him out. This she braced herself to do, eyes flashing and lips thinned in displeasure.

"What about the game of—post office?" he taunted as twin flames lighted the stygian darkness of his eyes.

"What about allowing me to pass," she retorted grimly. "I do have a job to do, you know."

"Teaching those precocious little mantraps how to draw? Forget it, honey—they could probably teach you a few things."

"It may come as a surprise to you, Donovan, but MCV is a vocational school, not an art school! It's no business of yours if I teach Swiss yodeling, but as it happens, I teach computer sciences." Which was stretching the truth just a bit. She taught word processing, mainly, with an occasional foray into smart typewriters and transcribing machines.

The look on his face was priceless. She reveled in the array of emotions she saw mirrored there until it occurred to her what was behind them. "You don't think I'm *capable* of teaching a business class?" she challenged, actually beginning to enjoy the thrust and feint of the confrontation.

"Let's just say I'm . . . surprised," he admitted. "I wouldn't have thought you were temperamentally suited for the more exact sciences." He raised a callused palm when sparks began to fly from her eyes. "Not that I underestimated you, honey, but in spite of your"—his eyes skimmed swiftly over her severly arranged hair, the unadorned beige shirtwaist and the plain tan pumps —"your disguise. But I've seen the real Grace Spencer, don't forget."

"It may come as news to you, Mr. Donovan, but this *is* the real Grace Spencer." She was about to wind up her case with a clincher to the effect that he had an outdated, chauvinistic, one-dimensional view of women, when they were interrupted by Carly Johns.

"Hi, Miss Spencer. Did you have a good holiday?" Carly had been absent the first day back at school, and Grace turned to her now with something of relief. "Wonderful, Carly. How was yours? You weren't ill yesterday, were you?"

"Oh, no, ma'am. We went to Disney World and we didn't get in until last night." Her eyes, soft as melted chocolate, kept drifting toward Donovan, and Grace had no choice but to introduce them. This she did, keeping it brief and to the point, but Quinn was not to be dismissed.

"Johns, huh? Charley Johns' little girl?" When Carly nodded, her face glowing like a neon sign under her orange hair, he went on to tease her with that no-fail charm of his. "I don't know how old Charley managed to have a daughter as pretty as you are, but I'll bet he has to sweep the boys off the doormat when he comes home from work every day."

He *had* to turn it on for anything in skirts! It was an automatic reflex! It was also unforgivable, Grace decided, when she saw the effect of his outrageous flattery on the impressionable girl. Her derisive glance told him as much, and he bathed them both in the indiscriminate warmth of his wide grin—the *phony* warmth, Grace preferred to think. "Well, if you two lovely ladies will excuse me, I have an appointment with a county official who's dead set on hogtyin' me with red tape."

"We'll try to bear up, Donovan," Grace retorted dryly, stepping around his intimidating bulk to reach the narrow gate.

"You do that, Spencer," he taunted softly. She received the full battery of his attention now, to her acute discomfort. Her lips tightened and she watched the unholy gleam rise up in his eyes to mock her. Beside her, Carly heaved a sigh of dramatic proportions as he turned to saunter across the cracked pavement to the blue truck. It was several moments before Grace could shake off the effects of his spell, and as she did she happened to catch Carly's eye with a rueful grimace. To her surprise the younger girl's smile held the first note of real communication they had shared. It *would* have to be over Donovan! Still, it was a beginning.

"Oh, wow, what a man," Carly breathed reverently as they followed the narrow concrete walk past a venerable magnolia tree. "Is he really for real, or not?"

"If he's not, then the sooner his batteries run down, the safer we'll all be," Grace admitted, holding the door for the student to enter.

Before they turned toward the classroom, Carly hesitated and Grace looked at her questioningly. This first tentative overture, the first sign of a thawing, was extremely fragile, and in spite of its ironic basis she was determined to foster it.

"Look, Miss Spencer—some of the girls—well, we thought it would be a neat trick to—" She broke off, her face flooding with color, and Grace glanced past her to see several of her students hurrying toward the room. "I'll tell you later," Carly mumbled and fled inside, leaving Grace to greet the others with a little less reserve than usual.

Whatever confidence Carly was about to share with her had to wait. Elliot came by at lunchtime and lingered until she was ready to go to the cafeteria, just as if he'd never snipped off their friendship. She'd just as soon he wouldn't try to put it back together again; she could do without Celia's charming attentions.

The reason for his seemingly casual visit became evident when he began to pump her about Jill.

Poor Elliot. She answered his questions, not offering any hopes that Jill would favor them with her presence again in the near future. "She really can't afford to be away from New York, Elliot. The competition's fierce in her profession, and she's only been with this agency a few months. In all the time I've been here in Brunswick, this is the first time she's visited me, so don't imagine she'll pop up every weekend or so." May as well squelch any hopes in that direction right off the bat.

Elliot sugared and stirred his coffee for the third time, and Grace found herself feeling unaccountably sorry for him. "Now and then I need to run up to New York," he murmured. "If you have any messages, I'd be glad to deliver them for you."

"Thanks Elliot. If I ever do, I'll let you know," she said, trying to keep the sympathy from her voice. Maybe she'd invent something. It might serve Jill right to have a few of her lovesick chickens come home to roost. "Are you going to have dessert?"

Poor Elliot. He was just as much a product of his upbringing as she was of hers, and neither of them was particularly adept at managing their personal relationships. Still, Jill and Celia notwithstanding, she had no intention of slipping back into a dating relationship with him.

Wait until you're asked, she rebuked herself, returning to the line for a slice of pecan pie. She got one for

Elliot, too, and turned the conversation to the latest shop rumor about frozen salaries. "They overextended themselves on that fancy new building," Elliot declared vindictively. "Donovan will get *his* money, never fear, even if the rest of us have to go on food stamps!"

Grace hurriedly finished her pie, unwilling to discuss Donovan in any way, shape or form, but Elliot was wound up. "I know you were hurt by the way I acted that night, Grace, but you see, you just don't understand, not being from around here."

"Please, Elliot, it really doesn't matter. I've forgotten—"

He wouldn't allow her to finish. Mouth full of pie, he said earnestly, "It never pays to get too friendly with the wrong types, Grace. You have your position here at MCV to think of, you know. Mother was horrified when I told her that that oaf was trying to start up something with you."

By degrees the sympathy she had felt for him was draining away, to be replaced by anger. "Elliot, It's really none of—"

"He's trash, Grace, nothing but pure trash. His father was run over by a train back in the fifties—dead drunk, as usual—and his mother was a cropper's daughter from Mississippi."

Grace stood up, her face pale with indignation on behalf of a man she didn't even like. "Did anyone ever tell you, Elliot Rand, that you were a first-rate snob? No, don't bother to get up. I'm going back to the room now. Oh, and by the way, there's a piece of pecan between your front teeth."

By the time her last class was over, she was through hyperventilating, although now and then, when she recalled Elliot's despicable attempt to belittle Donovan, she caught herself sucking in great gasps of air. All right! So the man was a conceited, irritating, sweet-talking womanizer! That had nothing to do with what his parents were or were not. Now that she thought about it, hadn't he told her that three of his four brothers had finished college, with the fourth joining the Coast Guard out of high school? And the girls—one was a nurse and the other happily married to a commercial fisherman. And Donovan himself had a perfectly good engineering degree from Georgia Tech. None of them had ended up on the streets, and if their father had died back in the fifties, when most of them would have been mere children, then at least a small part of the credit must be due to Donovan, as the oldest of the brothers.

"Rats," she seethed, throwing her briefcase into the front seat of her car. She had enough problems of her own without shouldering any of Donovan's!

As it turned out, she had a problem she hadn't counted on. Oh, her job was secure enough. For some reason the morning girls were on their best behavior. Even Terri seemed almost subdued, although whenever she attempted to renew that momentary flash of communication with Carly, the younger girl managed to evade her. She actually seemed embarrassed. Shrugging, Grace dismissed it. After all, there were at least a dozen years separating her from her students, practically a whole generation, and as long as they all seemed content to settle down to work, why ask for anything more?

No, the problem was Donovan. Being a landlord wasn't enough for him. Now, it seemed, he had decided to bring the rental house up to standards instead of tearing it down. He turned up on her doorstep at seven thirty-one on Saturday morning in mid-January with the unsettling news.

"It occurred to me, Grace, that with the price of a house well out of most folks' reach, it's downright wasteful to destroy one that could be put into first-class shape with a little elbow grease."

She stood there blinking at him, her cotton pajamas rumpled around her sleep-warmed body and her tousled braid half undone. "Have you gone stark—"

"Stark naked or stark, ravin' mad?" he completed, that impossibly guileless grin splitting his face wide open. Grace shuddered with impotent fury and attempted to slam the door shut, but he was too quick for her. "Ah, ah, ah—temper, Miss Spencer," he remonstrated gently.

Closing her eyes in a wordless prayer, Grace spun away and strode into her bedroom, slamming the door so that every picture on the wall banged against the white-painted paneling. Etched on her retina was an image of that king-sized creature surrounded by Aunt Aldonia's crocheted antimacassars and delicate china figurines.

It was the sound of drawers being opened and closed in the kitchen that finally drew her out of hiding. She had taken time to change into jeans and a peach-colored sweatshirt, but she needed to wash up and that meant running the gauntlet to get to the bathroom.

Up the standards, indeed! It would take more than a lick of paint and a few snide remarks to bring this old house up to even minimum standards, and anyway, she wasn't at all sure she wanted it improved. Over the past few months she had been able to vent a lot of ire on its shortcomings, thus saving her from exploding when the frustrations at school threatened to boil over. It was one thing to swear a blue streak at a door that refused to stay either open or closed, or a drawer that was stuck at the halfway point—quite another to speak her mind to the school administrator or a roomful of noisy, inattentive teenagers. She might shiver in an unheated bathroom during a cold, rainy spell, or keep a pair of rubber-soled shoes in the kitchen for times when the floor was too damp to be safe with electric appliances, but if improvement meant having to put up with Donovan, then she'd opt for the status quo.

He was making coffee when she charged, head down, through the kitchen to get to the bathroom. Some time later she emerged, feeling somewhat more refreshed, and confronted him, arms crossed over her breasts. "All right, Donovan, suppose we get down to business. If you're bound to go through with this farce, I'll give you a list of needed improvements and you can pass them on to your workmen. They can start on the outside first, and I'll arrange a schedule with them for doing the inside. I'm not about to go off and leave a crew of clumsy roughnecks in my house!" Wordlessly she dared him to reject her ultimatum.

He handed her a cup of coffee, and because the aroma was irresistible, she took it. Except for a certain look of pure devilment in his obsidian eyes, she would have sworn his smile was genuine. "All done now, little darlin'?" he asked solicitously.

"Donovan, if you call me little darling, or . . . or honey, or Pigtails one more time, I'm going to clobber you!" Her fist, curled around the warm mug, shook threateningly, sloshing coffee dangerously near the rim.

He put his own large hand over hers, drawing her into the living room and down onto the sofa. "I do enjoy a fine display of fireworks. You're a feisty little lady, aren't you? Must have something to do with your bein' a Yankee. All that ice in your system comes in contact with my manly southern warmth and—"

Trembling, she seethed, "I'll manly southern warmth you, you—! Get out of here, Donovan. It's not going to work! I'd sooner live in a dugout canoe than have to put up with your overbearing, condescending, *cornpone charm!"*

He applauded softly, leaning back in her one really good chair. "Your vocabulary's coming right along, little—Grace," he amended. "Keep it up and I might wind up sending you a bouquet of roses and daisies." He grinned at her, his eyes lazy-lidded and deceptively slumberous.

Closing her mind to the sheer physical magnificence of the man, Grace took a deep, steadying breath and began again, this time keeping her voice deliberately soft, as if she were dealing with a backward five-year-old. "Look, Mr. Donovan—Quinn, there are a few improvements I'd really like to see made—the bathroom, for instance, and maybe the kitchen door, but other than that, I'd just as soon you left things the way they are. I'm planning to stay here as long as I'm in Brunswick—or at least as long as the place is available, so you don't need to make a big deal of renovating it just for me. I'm satisfied, do you understand? I really like it just the way it is. Well . . . almost." She waited for him to reply, her spurious poise quickly deserting her as he continued to regard her with benign speculation. After the silence had spun out to a point almost beyond bearing, he shifted his weight in the blue-and-white-striped armchair.

"Suppose we do the rounds now, and you can point out anything that needs attention. Meanwhile, I'll look things over from a structural angle, and we'll work out a schedule that's agreeable to both of us. Fair enough?"

Her brain flipped through the words, searching for the catch. "Fair enough," she agreed reluctantly.

"Over breakfast."

Rising in one swift, graceful motion, she frowned down at him warily. "Over breakfast?"

"You haven't eaten yet, have you? Neither have I. I got two phone calls before seven this morning, and I decided to get out of the office and tackle a problem I stood a chance of solving with my own two hands. I left your number with Margaret, though, in case anything important comes up and I'm out of hearing of the mobile unit."

"Why? What gave you the idea you'd be here for any length of time? What if I hadn't been home? What business do you have giving out my private number to every Tom, Dick and Harry?"

"There you go again. Old Faithful, spoutin' off questions without giving a man time to think, much less speak." He stood up, reaching for her mug. "Better let me take that out to the kitchen for you. You seem to be a mite upset about something."

Upset! That was the understatement of the year! Just the sight of that impossibly smug grin of his, the sound of his sugar-coated blarney, was enough to make her come up swinging! Taking a deep breath, she spoke with deliberate calmness. "The floor of the little porch between the kitchen and the bathroom gives whenever I step on a certain board, and there's a . . . a sort of growth that comes along the baseboard in the kitchen and bathroom whenever we have a long, wet spell."

They toured the house, inside and outside, and Grace bit her tongue and averted her eyes when Quinn opened her bedroom closet to locate the access panel for the bathroom plumbing. To her over-exercised imagination, he seemed to spend three times as long studying that and the sticking window in her bedroom as he did the loose flashing around the chimney or the rotten sills under every porch.

By the time they wound up the survey, her stomach was rumbling. Quinn headed for the phone on her bedside table, grinning at her over his shoulder. "Why don't you fix us some breakfast, honey, and I'll just check in with Margaret and see if anything's come up."

Grace could hear every word. The drawling baritone seeped through the thin old wooden walls as if they weren't there. She put on four strips of bacon to sizzle while she whipped up four eggs. At least she could cook a creditable breakfast.

"Tell Monroe I'll call him about the Blalock bid Monday morning, first thing. I'll handle the bank at this end, but—yeah, that's right. Good!"

The bacon drained on a paper towel and Grace warmed two plates while she ran buttered bread under the broiler—which worked on an occasional basis.

"That's right, Maggie, but double-check to be sure it's marine grade. No, the specs won't be done for a week yet, but I want to be ready to move fast."

The eggs went into a buttered skillet and Grace stirred, aware of a strange desire to smile. She caught herself humming under her breath as Quinn's voice grated out a string of numbers, and then she stopped, instinctively aware of a subtle change of intonation.

"Sure, honey, you knock off about twelve, then. First, though, get ahold of those Blalock figures, will you? I'll pick you up about seven thirty. See you."

Grace slid a spoonful of eggs and two slices of bacon on each of the plates and thumped them down on the tiny metal table in a corner of the kitchen. She poured coffee in the mugs they had used earlier, pouring carelessly and then cursing when she slopped some across the tabletop.

"The toast is almost ready," she snapped. "Sit down!"

"Yes, ma'am."

She glared at him suspiciously, looking for mockery, and saw only his quickly suppressed look of dismay when he took his place before the large flowered plate with the two small strips of bacon and the spoonful of scrambled eggs. She reached into the oven, retrieved the two slices of toast and dropped them on his plate. "I don't eat toast," she lied, picking up her fork.

Ten minutes later Quinn headed out to his truck, mumbling something about picking up a few things from the shop. "Be back in half an hour," he called over his shoulder.

Grace turned to the sink, plunging her arms in and then leaning on the edge, staring down at the popping bubbles. She had forgotten how much a grown man could put away, although the men in her own family were inclined to be more moderate, both in size and in appetite. Poor Donovan had probably gone to a restaurant to supplement her meager offering.

He returned with both arms full of groceries. Grace held her tongue until he opened her refrigerator to put away a gallon of milk. "Would you mind telling me just what's going on here? Have you lost your mind?"

"Well, now, honey, I don't expect you to feed me just because I'm here working at your house," he informed her reasonably enough.

"Your house, you mean! You're not doing *me* any favors, and anyway, I thought your crew was going to do the actual work."

"I don't work 'em over the weekend. Man needs a little R and R."

"Oh, and when do you propose to have your own rest and recreation?" she jeered in saccharine tones. "Donovan, you know something? You irritate me considerably!"

He put away two dozen eggs and a pound of bacon and turned to bestow on her that beautiful, benevolent smile that drove her up the wall. "Don't worry about me, honey. I manage to get all the recreation a grown man needs, and as for irritating you, why, a little grain of sand irritates an oyster, too. And you know what comes of that, don't you?"

Fighting Quinn Donovan was like punching against the fog! How could any man be so helpful, so unfailingly good-humored—her mind shied away from the searing words he had left her with not too long ago—and *still* be so infuriating? The only way she could deal with his disrupting presence in her home was to leave, and this she did, gathering her portfolio and slamming out the front door.

By the time she returned, driven by hunger and the frustration of not being able to concentrate on her work, he was gone, and she resolutely denied the quick shaft of disappointment she felt.

The following week went quickly, with several shy overtures from her students. Terri still managed to throw her off balance with a knowing look and a sly smile, but Grace had learned to ignore it, for the most part. The colonel had his way of dealing with malcontents—she had to devise her own, and if it included ignoring what she couldn't change, then so be it.

On Friday night she went to a movie alone. Elliot and Celia were waiting in line for tickets, and Elliot's handsome face turned bright pink. He offered her a brief mumble by way of greeting, and Celia's smirk rolled harmlessly off her back. Grace's mind, unfortunately, was occupied with a certain outrageously attractive civil engineer who might or might not turn up on her doorstep in time for breakfast on Saturday.

At six thirty the following morning, with the sun still hidden behind a low-lying bank of clouds, Grace peered out her front window and then hurried to the bathroom to run herself a tub. She tossed in copious handfuls of bath salts and later dried herself and dusted down with a wildflower-scented talc before putting on a new pair of lavender jeans and a thin purple shirt. She left her hair hanging, brushing it until it flew about her head like amber rain.

Donovan showed up precisely at seven thirty, and she greeted him with a scowl. "Have you had breakfast?" she asked grudgingly.

"Not yet. I thought I might fix us one of my special KSO omelets." He tossed his worn Stetson on the table in the front room, skillfully avoiding the pompous cactus plant.

"KSO?" She *had* to ask, as he knew darned well she would. It was frightening, the way this man could manipulate a woman and actually turn her into an eager victim.

"Kitchen sink omitted," he obliged, beaming down at her a grin she chose to think of as fatuous.

"You're cute, Donovan—just too cute for words," she snapped, turning to lead the way to the kitchen. The door, as usual, hung halfway open and she gave it a shove that sent it clattering against the wall.

"We'll fix that after breakfast," he promised her as he set about removing the contents of her refrigerator.

The omelet was superb. He had used almost all the leftovers she had accumulated, binding them in a piquant sour cream and cheese sauce that was beyond belief. She cleaned her plate, forking the last tiny shrimp and wiping it in the perfectly seasoned sauce, and then stood and began to run water in the sink. "I'll get these done before I leave."

"Where are you going?" he asked with perfect equanimity.

Agitating the suds into snowy mounds, she applied herself to her chore. "I don't think that's any business of yours."

"You think I'm being too personal?" He reached around her and slid his dishes into the sink, and she flinched at his touch. It was like an electric shock. Her breath caught somewhere behind her solar plexus, and it was a moment before she could answer.

"Look Donovan, I make it a policy not to mix business with pleasure. I'm sure you've found, as I have, that it's far better to keep one's relationships properly separated. You're here to work and that's as far as it goes. Maybe you'd better have breakfast before you get here next week—that is," she hesitated, "if you come back next week." She scrubbed furiously at the innocuous blue rose that centered the old yard-sale china plate.

The silence stretched the boundaries of comfort to the breaking point before Quinn replied. "You call the shots, honey—I just try to accommodate you. Before you go, though, how about helping me with this door. It'll just take a minute to tighten up the hinges, and then I can get started on the back porch. Probably rain before evening, and I'd like to rip out the old wood before I knock off for the day."

She finished the dishes, leaving them to drain, and presented herself to Quinn, who was doing something with a folding rule and a plumb bob. "All you have to do is lean against it while I replace these old screws with longer ones. Wood's so dry they've pulled out." He positioned her where he wanted her and busied himself selecting a screwdriver from the open toolbox on the floor. Grace stared down at the thick crop of soft, dark curls and fought against an insane desire to touch them.

He stood up and moved in toward the doorjamb, bracing himself with one arm while he deftly replaced the screws. He was so close that she could feel his breath against the side of her averted face. "Why can't you just prop it closed with a chair?" she asked plaintively.

Without turning his head, he muttered something

unintelligible and then stood back, dropped the screwdriver into the toolbox and turned to her. "Because, my lapis-eyed darlin', a chair's not nearly as exciting as a carpenter's helper."

By the time she managed to break the paralysis that had set in, it was too late. It had been too late all along. One large arm moved to pin her in place as he stepped in front of her. When she tried to duck under his elbow, he blocked her with his body, pressing her heavily against the door.

"Quinn, behave yourself!" She adopted her best schoolmarm tone and heard it come out as a breathless whisper.

"Not now, Grace—behaving myself is the farthest thing from my mind." His face moved across her own in tantalizing slow motion. The proud thrust of his nose stroked the tip of hers, and his mustache brushed over her lips, her cheeks. When she could no longer bear the fibrillation of her own distraught nerves, she moved that necessary fraction of an inch to find his mouth with hers. It was a sweet, mutual coercion that melted the last vestige of her resistance.

If he had only meant to make a teasing sort of gesture, it failed badly. Quinn evidently had no more control over his reactions than Grace did, and in mere seconds tension had spread through his hard-muscled body, igniting a similar response in hers. His mouth lifted, trailed to her throat, and he groaned against the silky, sensitive flesh. "Ahhh, Grace, Grace, you're full of surprises, aren't you? When are you going to share the sweetest secret of all with me?"

Pulses that were all but out of control froze for an instant, and then, at the feel of his hand inside her shirt, stroking her breast into a tiny volcano of burning need, she closed her mind to all but the growing tumult in her body. Fumbling fingers located the buttons of his crisp khaki shirt and made swift work of them, sliding upward to comb through the pelt on his chest. He stiffened as her fingers raked his flat, male nipples, and after a moment when neither of them seemed able to draw a breath, he caught at her hand and moved it inexorably downward.

"Honey, no more games—please. A man can only stand so much and stay sane."

Sane! What was sanity? The world spun wildly around a holocaust that was burning out of control, and sanity was quenching it in the age-old way, the only way possible, before it consumed them both!

He thrust a knee between her thighs, lifting her to hold her against him as his tongue traced a sensuous pattern on her throat, flickering over the frantic pulse. Slowly, as if her neck were too delicate to bear the weight of her head, she lowered her face to bury it in his hair—it was soft, warm, vital, like the man himself. A faint warning echo tried to remind her that there was nothing at all soft about Quinn, nothing vulnerable as she was vulnerable; she closed her mind to it, blocking out all but the hands that were moving over her, skillfully loosening her clothes, shucking her out of them as if she were a tender ear of corn.

Her shirt slithered to the floor, followed by the lacy wisp of her bra. Quinn gazed down at the coral-tipped ivory of her breasts, his usual smile a tense parody of itself. His eyes were hidden, a faint flush stained his sharp-edged cheekbones and Grace felt an irrational desire to tear off the rest of her clothes and offer herself totally, freely. Surely it was wrong to deny such a cataclysmic need?

Once more her head drooped, and he caught the tip of her chin and lifted her face to his. "Your eyes, Grace, are as black as mine now. You can't deny the truth anymore than I can."

His words, spoken in a hoarse whisper, so nearly echoed her own thoughts that Grace closed her eyes in relief. No, she couldn't deny it—didn't want to deny the power that surged between them like an arcing high-tension line. It was far stronger than reason. It obliterated all logic—it was quite simply undeniable.

"Kiss me now, Grace, and tell me what you want. The time for games is past."

Drawn as inevitably as steel to a magnet, she closed the few inches between them, her lips moist and parted for his invasion, and when the phone shrilled in the next room she blinked slowly, unable to understand for a moment what was happening. Leave it! she wanted to cry out, but the fierce tension was broken now, and a shred of sanity fingered its way in through overwrought emotions.

"I'll take it off the hook," Quinn grated, eyes flashing frustration.

"No, I—that is, I'd better get it." Reacting instinctively, she slid away and grabbed up her shirt, struggling to get her arms through the inverted sleeves. She received very few calls of a personal nature and it could be one of her family. Besides, she needed time—time to think before she committed herself to something she might regret for the rest of her life.

"Give me Quinn," a terse feminine voice demanded, and Grace stared stupidly down at the instrument, trying to bring her mind to bear on the intrusion of reality. For it was reality—whoever the unknown woman was, she had saved Grace from making a fool of herself. For a few wild, impossible moments she had almost forgotten that a man . . . a man like Quinn . . .

"What is it? Grace? Who is it?" he demanded. His voice sounded raspy, as if it had not been used in a long time.

"It's for you—a woman," she said dully. She laid the

phone carefully on the table and moved away, shoving her shirttail into the waist of her jeans.

Quinn bit off an oath and brushed past her. She could feel the angry energy radiating from him as he snatched up the receiver and barked into it.

"The devil you say! Did he give a reason?" A pause, and then a gruff order. "Tell him the original figures stand! If he wants a court battle, I can handle it a damned sight better than he can!"

There was no softness in evidence now—no hint of the easygoing charm in that deep, southern drawl. He was all fire and steel, and Grace closed her ears to the sound of Quinn's succinctly phrased orders. Before she could weaken and change her mind, she snatched up her purse and her portfolio and ran out the door.

Quinn made no attempt to stop her.

Chapter Seven

Grace left her car just across the bridge in Darien and walked along the wharves, staring absently at the trawlers there, all bristling with esoteric superstructure. After a while she found an uninhabited stretch of marshfront, similar to the marshland some fifteen miles farther south in Brunswick. At least there was no danger of running into Quinn here. Had she sought refuge in her own private sanctuary at the end of the road that went past her house, he might have found her.

Ha! Some ego she'd acquired! As if he'd be hot on her trail as soon as he hung up the phone! He was probably prying away at the back porch with a crowbar right this minute—either that or still slamming out orders to that sexy-voiced female. And to think she had once considered him a simple bulldozer operator—one of a dozen or so construction workers who had made her days a nightmare!

She'd forget him. Forget him and get on with her life, with her work. Unfortunately it wasn't going to be particularly easy, she thought with resigned self-knowledge. It seemed that she had a flaw in her makeup, a secret vulnerability that no amount of good intentions would protect.

Deliberately shutting out the haunting beauty of the mysterious marshes, she tried to concentrate on composing a verse for a Christmas card, but all that would come to mind were inane jingles about hearts and flowers.

> *Daisies have a secret;*
> *Roses have one, too.*
> *Listen with your heart, my dear,*
> *They'll tell you I love you.*

Good Lord, what had made her remember that one? It had been one of her first attempts at doing valentines—she had all but forgotten it. But Quinn had mentioned roses and daisies—purely a coincidence—but it had obviously been enough to trigger her subconscious. She'd just have to force herself to forget valentines and think fall—think Thanksgiving, think Halloween!

It started to sprinkle, and by the time she found her way back to her car, she was thoroughly soaked. Just as well she hadn't gotten involved in anything important. Once she latched onto a theme, she tended to keep after it compulsively, like a dog with a bone, but if her train of thought was interrupted, she had a terrible time trying to get back with it.

Halloween. All she could come up with was an image of wicked, dark eyes topped with Mephistophelian brows. In spite of herself, she smiled. How would Quinn like to see his face adorning a series of scary cards?

Thanksgiving? She couldn't quite see him as an early Puritan. All the same, there was something essentially —for want of a better word, she came up with "good" —about Quinn Donovan. Integrity, reliability, even kindness; all highly desirable qualities in any man. Odd that in spite of all that, she couldn't bring herself to trust him.

The note was in the front room, under the begonia pot, and she almost missed it in the premature gloom. Dropping her things on the arm of a tapestry-padded Mission oak chair, she switched on the ugly overhead fixture and in the cold glare of its single bulb read the heavily scrawled words.

"Sorry you had to leave just when we were having so much fun mixing business with pleasure." It was signed "QED." Grace uttered an unladylike oath, crumpled it into a ball and tossed it at the pristine wastepaper basket for which Aunt Aldonia had crocheted a green slipcover.

QED, indeed! *Quod erat demonstrandum.* If she remembered correctly from her long-ago skirmish with geometry, that was Latin for "which was to be demonstrated." As far as *she* was concerned, it had meant, "There! I've finally solved your stupid old problem!"

Only she was just now coming to realize how far she was from solving the problem of QED.

Time was the balm that soothed the injured surface of her ego, and it took the edge off the raw wanting that Quinn had aroused in the depths of her. By the middle of the following week Grace had her priorities all in proper sequence, and Quinn wasn't even on the list.

Brunswick was bedeviled by fog. It burned off during the day, only to return with evening, laying over the marshes and rivers like ragged gossamer scarves. She reread Lanier's *Marshes of Glynn* and stared morosely out over the silent, evocative sea of rushes.

Inward and outward to northward and southward
The beach-lines linger and curl
As a silver-wrought garment that follows and clings
To the firm sweet limbs of a girl.

It seemed that everything was conspiring to put her in an unbearably romantic frame of mind. It took an almost heroic effort to attach her mind to her work, but Grace managed to get through whole hours without once thinking of Donovan. On Wednesday she had arranged a trip to several offices that utilized a variety of transcribing machines, dictaphones and word processors. Some of the advanced secretarial students were already branching out into the various professional terminologies, and this trip was designed to acquaint the younger girls with the endless possibilities for application of their new skills.

The law firm that had agreed to receive a small group had its offices in a complex that also housed several medical practices, making it ideal to conduct the two groups at once. While the law firm's receptionist was describing the glamorous possibilities of working as a legal secretary and then taking further training to become a paralegal, an attractive office manager was conducting the other group through the complex that made up the Medical Arts Center.

Grace, with half an hour to herself, arranged to meet the two groups at a nearby fast-food place and pushed through the heavy glass doors, squinting against the low-angled morning sun. Barely had the doors swung behind her than she felt herself pinioned by both shoulders, and then an arm slid around her back and Quinn grinned down at her—an unfamiliar Quinn, wearing a vastly becoming three-piece suit. The gray at his temples, instead of merely adding to his rakish good looks, lent an even greater air of dignity.

"Playing Mother Goose this morning?"

"Playing Mother . . . ? Oh, I see what you mean." She answered his flashing smile with a reluctant one of her own—one that faded swiftly as she saw his eyes sweep over her in a practiced inventory.

Stiffening against the familiar arm that had dropped to her waist, she pulled away. "Well, it was nice seeing you, Quinn, but I must rush. I—the—my classes . . ." She wallowed lamely, her eyes unconsciously pleading to be released from the magnetism of his gaze. If anything, he was even more stunning than she remembered in a suit that had obviously been expertly tailored to his dynamic proportions.

"Have coffee with me," he commanded genially.

"I really don't have time."

"What were you planning to do while your little ducklings are being initiated into the mysteries of the real world?"

Stung by his derisive dismissal of her girls, she said, "My little ducklings, as you call them, are what make the so-called real world go around! I doubt very much that QD Engineering would function as smoothly without its office staff!"

"Margaret." And at her mystified look, he said, "My office staff—Margaret Phillers. Which reminds me, I'm having a get-together Friday evening, in the part of my house that's finished. I'd like for you and that friend of yours—forget his name, but the one with the nose designed to be looked down."

"Elliot," she said before she could stop herself, and then, at Quinn's easy rumble of laughter, she felt her hands curling into impotent fists. "That wasn't fair, Quinn, nor was it nice!"

"No, honey, I guess it wasn't, but you didn't have any trouble recognizing him from the description, did you? Come on now, don't go all huffy on me, like a broody little bantam hen. I really do want the two of you to come out to my party." His face took on an expression that, in a lesser man, might have been taken for wistfulness. "I've been a little too busy over the past half dozen or so years to cultivate many friends, so when I feel in the mood to celebrate, I need 'em all—every one of 'em."

Grace's heart lurched painfully. She wanted to gather him to her, all six-feet-three, two hundred plus pounds of him, and soothe away any hurts that had been inflicted by the harshness of his early years. "Of course we'll come, Quinn," she assured him, her voice rich with feeling, and his hand wrapped around her own two clasped ones, squeezing them tightly.

"I knew I could count on you, honey," he beamed. "About seven-thirty, all right? See you!" He spun away, leaving a mesmerized Grace staring after him, wondering if she had imagined the gleam of triumph that had been swiftly submerged under the opaque surface of his eyes. Wondering, too, when she was ever going to grow up. Most children learned not to lay hands on a hot stove after the first experience.

She hesitated to ask Elliot, but he and Celia didn't seem quite so close just lately. Maybe she'd be doing him a favor; if the librarian thought he was lapsing back to his old habits with Grace, she might come around.

At first he refused even to consider it. Then, when he realized Grace was going, either with or without him, he capitulated, telling her that for old time's sake he couldn't allow her to go to Donovan's house unescorted. His carefully controlled look of distaste was a clear indication that he suspected the worst, and Grace decided Quinn hadn't been all that far out in his description of Elliot's nose—its thin tip fairly quivered with indignation at the idea of her being exposed to Donovan's decadent influence.

In a burst of extravagance Grace bought herself a silky white knit with an unusual wide, square neckline. It made the most of her creamy coloring and her long, delicate bones. Tilting her head to study the effect, she regretted the lack of a suitable bit of costume jewelry to enhance the unrelieved garment. The lily goes ungilded, she sighed, admiring the clearly defined angle of her jawline. It was firm, if decidedly feminine. "You're no pushover, Spencer, no matter what anyone says. You're not old Ironbottom Spencer's daughter for nothing, you know."

Elliot, punctual to the minute, had forgone his tweeds for the pinstripe, with the perennial black knit tie. He approved Grace's appearance with a brief, smug nod and sniffed suspiciously at the drift of subtle perfume. "If you're ready, we may as well go," he informed her. *Into the valley of death rode the four hundred,* Grace interpreted. Aloud she murmured, "Or was it six hundred?" and had Elliot stare at her as if she were demented. She shrugged a beige mohair stole around her shoulders and smiled at him.

It hadn't occurred to her that she might have trouble finding Quinn's place again, but she needn't have worried. Elliot took all the correct turns with no advice from her. "You haven't been here before, have you?" she asked when he turned off onto the long, shelled driveway. Lights were filtering through the soughing pines.

"Everyone knows where Scarp Bluff is. It was one of the most desirable properties on the mainland until Donovan mysteriously came into possession of it. Quite a change from a shotgun shanty overrun with brats and mongrels!"

Grace closed her eyes momentarily, willing herself not to dignify the sneering innuendo with a reply. Donovan didn't need defending from the likes of Elliot

Rand. It was painfully clear that poor Elliot couldn't handle the fact that someone who hadn't his mother's seal of approval had managed to make the grade without it. In that respect he was more to be pitied than Donovan—and it occurred to her that Donovan was well aware of that fact.

There were several cars there besides Quinn's low-slung sports car—a rakish red British thing, an assortment of elegant luxury sedans and a slightly battered pickup truck. Elliot parked his own white Ford as far away from the latter as he could manage, and Grace suppressed a smile with difficulty. From somewhere outside she heard Mollie's greeting—a yap ending in a mournful howl—and then Quinn threw open the door for them, gesturing expansively for them to come join the others. "She wanted to come to the party," he explained in an undertone, nodding in the direction of the canine protest, "but I managed to bribe her with a slab of ribs." He slipped an arm around Grace's shoulders, relieving her of her wrap, and smiled as Elliot stepped warily inside to cast an anxious glance at the already assembled gathering.

Grace was reminded of the way Elliot reacted to her bevy of cats, as if expecting the worst at every step. This time she was unsuccessful in suppressing her smile, and Quinn immediately leaned nearer. "Glad you decided to come, Grace. I'd have been disappointed if you'd let a little misunderstanding come between us," he murmured for her ears alone.

Before she could come up with a single rational thought, much less a reply, a woman in a long, sleeveless shift of navy blue inserted herself between them. The same woman who had been with him at the supper club a month or so ago.

Grace's initial opinion of a rather hard prettiness was reinforced on closer inspection. Even as Quinn was

introducing her and Elliot to Margaret Phillers, Grace
was aware of several swift impressions; that the button-
front shift, which should have been innocuous enough
for anyone's taste, became something else altogether
on Miss Phillers, due partly to the fact that it was
unbuttoned a third of the way down and halfway up.
The second impression was just as swift and every bit as
powerful. Margaret Phillers was head over heels in love
with her boss and was determined that no other woman
was going to get within striking distance of him.

"Miss Spencer, Mr. Rand—help yourself to drinks
over there, and I'll introduce you around in just a
minute," the lean, cool-eyed woman said. "I need a
word with Quinn."

In other words, I'm hostess in Quinn's house, Grace
interpreted, unprepared for the swift shaft of pain that
shot through her as she watched Margaret Phillers slant
a confiding little smile up at her boss. Hooking her arm
through Elliot's, Grace more or less dragged him across
the long room to the table, extended for the occasion
and sumptuously spread, buffet style, with a variety of
dishes. Poor Elliot still looked as if he suspected the
cocktail sauce of having been prepared from a Borgia
recipe, but he was approached by an acquaintance—
evidently a socially acceptable one—and then several
people introduced themselves to Grace and the evening
began to gather momentum.

"Hi, you're Grace and I'm Edward, and I'm told
you're something of an artist yourself."

She turned to confront a broad grin that was a
younger, slightly lower voltage version of Quinn's.
Edward Donovan had the same unruly crop of curls,
but in a lighter shade. His eyes were as dark, but much
less compelling. "That's overstating the facts, I'm
afraid," she admitted, allowing her hand to be captured
and held for several moments. "I do colored drawings

—that's a world apart from painting, and we both know it."

"To each his own—to coin an old saying," Edward quipped, and offered to supplement her partly filled plate with a glass of wine. "Red, white or a delicate, blush-pink rosé?"

Allowing herself to be led across to a heavily cushioned daybed, she opted for white and then was offered a choice of still or sparkling.

"You choose," she laughed, carefully placing her plate on a handsome oak coffee table adorned with hammered copper corners. "I try not to make difficult decisions on an empty stomach."

While the party milled around them, Edward regaled her with the course of his career as an artist and inquired into Grace's own endeavors along that line. "I doodle," she admitted, "and am lucky enough to have found a market for some of my doodlings, but I've never considered myself an artist."

"Darling, art is a way of life, not a particular thing you do! Paintings, sculpture, music—mere by-products of that life," the young man said with an engaging shrug. "Seriously, Grace, don't put yourself down. Some of the best of us never make a dime at it and some of the rankest make a killing. So far no one's come up with a precise definition of art, much less laid down the specifications for a practitioner."

They were joined by another couple, and presently someone put on some music and a courtly gentleman she vaguely recognized as being a county commissioner asked her to dance.

It was quite late when Quinn came up behind her. She had been aware of him all night long, aware of his towering figure moving slowly around the room as he chatted first with one group, then another. The fact that she had managed to stay on opposite sides of the room from him was partly deliberate, partly instinctive. She was far too conscious of Elliot's narrowed gaze, as if he expected her at any moment to do something outrageous, nor was she unconscious of Margaret's speculative looks. Miss Phillers was an extremely attractive lady, as well as an extremely possessive one. When she wasn't actually demonstrating her possession of the tall, striking man in the white trousers, the black shirt and the velvety gray corduroy jacket, she was sending hands-off signals to every female in range, with special emphasis on Grace.

"You've been avoiding me," Quinn said behind her, his voice raising goosebumps down her spine.

"Now, why on earth should I bother to do that?" Grace managed with surprisingly well faked coolness. "Your ego's showing."

"Dance with me." He didn't permit her to refuse, drawing her skillfully into his arms as someone put on another tape.

She felt as if she were made of paper. Her limbs moved stiffly against his, threatening at any moment to buckle under her. She wasn't at all sure she could handle the physical contact, but Quinn was in complete control of the situation, reading the state of her nerves with uncanny accuracy.

"Relax," he rumbled against the top of her head. "I'm not going to eat you here."

"It's not *your* fangs I'm worried about," she retorted before she could stop herself.

"Not afraid of the big bad wolf?" he teased, swinging her tightly against him as they almost collided with another couple. There were only about a dozen couples there, but in what was essentially a one-room house, it was enough. She felt herself falling under the spell of his potent magnetism, prey to all the old familiar longings she had tried so hard to deny. She turned her head to one side and stared fixedly at one of Edward's more aggressive paintings, willing her hands not to caress, her breasts not to tingle and her legs not to be so piercingly aware of every subtle muscular movement as Quinn moved to the slow rhythm of the music.

"What do you think of Edward?"

"I liked him immensely."

"Not too immensely, I hope. He has a reputation among the ladies." They found themselves beside the sliding glass doors when the music ended, and Quinn led her through, out onto the open-sided corridor that led to the unfinished part of the building. "Come see my home," he invited, forestalling her crack about the pot and the kettle. Looking down at her in the light that came through the doors, he laughed. He knew perfectly well that she had been about to bring up his own flamboyant reputation with the women. Maybe it was nothing to be ashamed of, but he didn't have to be so darned arrogant about it! As if the women of the world were his garden and he was king bee.

He showed her through a jungle of rafters and joists, studs and empty window frames, identifying the various rooms. A quarter moon slanted down on them, angling under the finished roof, and Grace found it impossible not to examine every nuance of his deep, expressive voice for a clue to his real feelings. Had he conducted all the others through his unfinished home earlier tonight, or was she the chosen one, and if so, what did it mean?

"Watch that two-by-four," Quinn warned just as Grace caught her shin on it. She doubled over in pain and Quinn scooped her up, holding her against him even as he chided her for trying to race off on her own. She had reacted to her own skittish instincts, she supposed, in trying to get away from him before she did something irrevocably foolish, and now it was too late.

As the hands that held her shoulders began to slide down her back, bringing her unresisting form into his powerful magnetic field, she raised her head in mute surrender. She could have no more prevented his kiss than she could have held back the tides.

"Oh, my, you are a tantalizing—bewitching—intriguing little morsel," he whispered as he planted tiny kisses along her throat. His mustache, soft and bristly at the same time, tickled her sensitized skin. "When are you going to send me another love letter?"

Understandably enough, it took a while for the last part to get through. Tantalizing? Bewitching? Intriguing? Was that the same Grace Spencer she had lived with all these years? Besides, all her brain cells were occupied in assimilating the overload of sensory information—the taste of him on her tongue, the scent of him in her nostrils and the feel of the hand that had by now found her breast and was deliberately stroking the nipple into eager arousal. "Grace? Did you think I didn't know?"

Know what? The words ricocheted around in her mind, but the time to utter them came and went as the glass doors slid open and they were approached by at least half the party. Quinn spoke, his own voice showing no trace of the whirlwind of emotions that still affected her. He warned his guests about the various hazards. "Poor Grace has already lost a leg to one of my braces."

Somehow—and she was never quite certain afterward just how the transition came about—Elliot was on one side of her, taking over her support from Quinn, and Edward was on the other, insisting that she come inside and allow him to minister to her with brandy and cold compresses.

"Silly, I'm not quite a basket case yet," she laughed shakily. It hurt like the very devil, as a matter of fact, now that the other sensations were subsiding. "At worst, I've managed to ruin my hose and bruise my shin. I think a glass of your wine will take care of that, Edward." She couldn't look at Quinn. He had turned her over to his brother readily enough when Margaret came on the scene. Now that she thought about it, Grace was pretty certain that the auburn-haired girl had been leading the pack when they had come through the door and scented their quarry.

She hobbled back into the softly lighted room, and while Edward secured a cold cloth to ease her bruise, Elliot poured her a glass of wine. "Mind you, I personally think a cup of hot, sweet coffee would be better—you look terrible, Grace."

"Thanks," she retorted dryly. "That helps immensely."

"You know what I mean," he sulked, and then Edward was there, running an all-too-knowing eye over her pale face as he knelt to lay the compress over her shin.

The party broke up soon afterward, but not before Edward had invited her to attend the opening of his one-man show in Atlanta the following weekend.

"Hush now, honey! Don't tell me you can't make it. You're in no condition now to make any decisions, so why don't I give you a call tomorrow. Maybe we can get together and you can show me some of your own work. I'm going to be around until Tuesday, and then I have to dash back to start collecting things from the framer."

Grace was acutely conscious of Elliot's disapproving eyes on her as she tried to come up with an excuse. And then the phone rang and Margarget hurried in to answer it. She summoned Quinn as he was striding across the room to where Grace was, whispering something to him as she leaned against his shoulder.

Grateful for the chance to escape, Grace said a hasty

good night to Edward, asking him to pay her respects to her host. With her arm hooked securely in Elliot's, she hurried out to the familiar safety of his car.

Grace's impressions as they drove silently through thin drifts of moonlit fog were no less painful than the darkening bruise on her shin. In her confused state she was glad of Elliot's preoccupation—searching for an excuse to justify his own prejudice, no doubt, or perhaps he was looking for a way to rationalize Quinn's obvious success. It must rankle, to know that a man one considered less than the dirt under one's feet was owner of a fast-growing business and an impressive home, as well as being friends with a county commissioner, a tool-and-die tycoon and one of the area's leading contemporary historians.

Nor was Elliot the only one who had problems reconciling the different facets of Quinn Donovan's personality. The man was forever confusing her, showing her sides of himself that didn't jibe with her early preconception of a rough-and-ready bulldozer operator with a fast line for the women. Gradually her thoughts polarized on two facts; she was inescapably in love with Quinn Donovan, and he was the last man on earth she could trust with the keeping of her vulnerable heart.

He was too experienced, too sure of his own compelling attractiveness, too free with the casual endearments to be anything but an older, far more dangerous version of Don Franklin. She'd be asking for trouble if she ever allowed him to know the extent of her feelings. She'd be in his bed so fast—and probably out of it just as swiftly once the conquest was made. Men, and especially bachelors of Quinn's age, were notoriously wary when it came to anything that touched on commitment. A man like Donovan would want all the privileges of marriage and none of the responsibilities, just as Don had.

Elliot said a glum good night to her at her door. He hadn't even danced with her during the evening, not that she cared. Even without Celia, or his vain hopes where Jill was concerned, there was nothing there for her.

Edward called just as she was headed out the door the next morning. Not even to herself would she admit the depths of her disappointment when Quinn had failed to show up for breakfast. She had a question to ask him, and regardless of the warning bells clanging in her mind, it kept nagging at her. What had he meant last night when he asked when she was going to send him another love letter? Was it some obscure reference to the note *he* had left for *her?* Or a reference to the note she had sent through Ogleby about the kitchen-bathroom problem? But that was absurd!

He accused *her* of playing games—it seemed he was even more adept at it than she was, not that she had ever been good at anything of the sort. Too straightforward. Even in checkers, Bart had told her she was entirely too predictable. No subtlety whatsoever.

For several moments, on hearing Edward's voice suggesting that they meet for lunch, she had trouble dragging her attention back from the maze of her own thoughts. "Lunch," she repeated vacantly. "Sure. Why not?" It was ten, or thereabouts, and she had already wasted half the morning moping around. May as well shoot the works!

He apologized for taking her to an inexpensive chain restaurant, explaining that all his liquid assets were tied up in launching his most important exhibit to date. They ordered catfish sandwiches and fried dill pickles, a specialty of the house, and Grace found herself unexpectedly telling the young artist all about her work for All Seasons. "Tight little renditions, ticky-tacky jingles," she minimized self-consciously, and he insisted that they go back to her house so that he could see for himself.

Actually Grace always carried a copy of The Valentine in her purse, if only to reassure herself that she could do something besides operate a few cold, emotionless machines, but she was too embarrassed to admit it.

The afternoon evolved into one of the most pleasant she had spent in some time. Edward admired her house, exclaiming over the pure Victoriana in the front room and the abstract design of the room-sized rug she had created from sample bits and pieces. "It's my poor man's Mondrian," she admitted laughingly, "and if you'd care to see my Jackson Pollock, step into the kitchen. The linoleum was ancient, anyway, and when the surface wore off, I dribbled all of Uncle Henry's odds and ends of paint all over it."

They finished up half a bottle of flat wine and munched on the cheese straws Grace had made during a cooking binge earlier in the week. Edward read her verses, but considerately restricted his comments to the tiny initials, GBS, with which she signed them. "G. B. Shaw, I presume," he observed dryly.

"Would you believe Grace Blair Shakespeare?"

"I like your drawings—this old-fashioned looking valentine thing, especially. It has a fresh naiveté that's surprisingly effective," he told her, and she warmed pleasurably at the sincerity in his voice. "May I ask who inspires such palpating sentiments?"

"You may not," she replied witheringly. "Credit me with some imagination."

Unconvinced, he persisted. "What about my free-wheeling brother? You two raised a few eyebrows and at least one little ol' gal's blood pressure when you snuck out on the party last night. Poor Maggie was fit to be tied when the pair of you turned up missing."

His grin was as guileless as Quinn's at his best—or worst—and Grace knew with a sinking feeling that she was going to pump him shamelessly. "I guess if anyone has the right to be upset, she does," she murmured, and waited for a rebuttal.

"Could be. He took her in and gave her a job, straightened out the mess she had made of her life. Must have been, oh, four, five years ago." Edward shrugged. He was built along much more modest lines than his brother, but his shoulders in the velour pullover were nothing to be ashamed of. "As far as Maggie's concerned, Quinn walks on water."

Grace stared unseeingly at a ladybug who patrolled the rim of a flowerpot against aphids, and Edward, oblivious of her conflicting emotions, went on to explain why it was perfectly natural for any woman to feel that way about the eldest Donovan.

"You see, Quinn has this overgrown sense of responsibility. He was landed with a king-sized load of it before he was even out of high school. The old man bowed out, and Mama, bless her, wasn't up to dealing with a houseful of little blessings on less than nothing." His tone was casual, but it was obvious to Grace that the memory still chafed. She felt almost guilty for allowing him to continue, but Edward needed no prompting. He told of young Quinn's taking over the reins of the family, dragging them up to subsistence levels and beyond through pure guts and gall. Grace leaned forward, fascinated, and gazed raptly into the lean, attractive face that was a pale echo of Quinn's.

"There weren't all that many possibilities, not unless a man had a boat and a set of nets, but Quinn has talent for making the best of his options—always had. He didn't know a blessed thing about operating heavy equipment, but he knew there was money to be made. He hung around a construction site for about a week, conned some poor sucker into letting him have a go at it and the next Monday, bright and early, he presented himself to a small outfit as a heavy equipment operator. Learned in the saddle. Before he was done, he had put us all through school—of course, LeighAnn got married, but she had a first-class wedding, I can tell you that."

Edward's face reflected something of the admiration he felt for his brother, and Grace swallowed around the constricting lump in her throat.

"He dragged us up by our teeth and toenails, and let me tell you, if the occasion arose, he was more than able to apply a hand where it would do the most good. He waited until the last one of us was launched before he started putting himself through school, and by the time he finally got his degree, he knew more than most of his instructors—a devil of a lot more, when it came to practical experience."

A fleeting frown passed over Edward's attractive young features. "As far as I recall, he didn't have much time for his own pleasures back in those days. I seem to remember a girl—Allie, or something unusual like that. I guess it just didn't work out. The poor gal probably took one look at the responsibilities heaped on Quinn's shoulders and made tracks in a hurry. I wonder . . ." he mused, and then, shaking his head in dismissal of ancient history, "I was too wrapped up in my own affairs to pay much attention at the time, and Quinn's never mentioned her. Not that he would—not his style." Grace absorbed the truth of that statement and swallowed the questions that rushed to the surface of her mind.

"It took him about three years to put QD Engineering on the map as one of the top outfits in the state, and let me tell you something, Grace, if Maggie loves him, it's no more than he deserves. Quinn's a big man, in all respects, but his heart is the biggest part of him," he said, and Grace's throat ached at the emotional pride that shone in his eyes. "I love him more than I'll ever love anyone else—we all do. He's a man," he finished simply, and for a long while they just sat there, staring into the shaft of afternoon sunshine that filtered through the climbing plants in the window.

Chapter Eight

Preoccupied, Grace managed to get through the first half of the week without actually barging into any walls. Yet far too often she found her attention drifting away from the classroom, hovering like a dragonfly unwilling to commit itself to a landing site. Her work was suffering, both at school and at home, and there were times when she felt like reaching up and grabbing her wayward mind and shaking it into obedience. She couldn't *concentrate!*

She had been sleeping badly, eating not at all, and it showed. Any color her cheeks had once boasted had long since fled, leaving her with new hollows and haunted eyes—eyes she instinctively avoided meeting in her mirror.

On Wednesday she called the bus station and inquired about the round-trip fare to Atlanta. It would have to be buses and taxis; she didn't dare risk trying to get about that teeming metropolis under her own steam. At least she knew her own limitations. As for clothes, *if* she went, she'd have to take either the lavender georgette or her new white knit—and of the two, the white, bought especially for Quinn's party, would be more the suitable. Memories or no memories, she could ill afford any melodramatic gestures. Not with her already limited wardrobe.

The sooner she faced the facts of life, the better. Quinn was too darned large to ignore, especially in a town the size of Brunswick, and whether she wanted to or not, she was bound to see him from time to time. The trick was to put him into perspective. *Some trick!*

On Thursday she stood before the classroom window and stared absently out across the winter-weary grounds. January always seemed to go on forever, and February looked as if it would be no improvement. She *needed* a break. She needed the trip to Atlanta, and she was going. Quinn would be there; her silly, lemming-like heart surged at the thought. He'd lift a wicked brow, brandish that blinding smile of his and toss out a few honeys and a darlin' or two, and every woman in the room would have palpitations! And she'd melt in her tracks, just like all the other poor fools!

She could still back out. Just because she had promised Edward she'd be there. . . . He's probably have forgotten all about her by then.

On the other hand it was a terribly important occasion for him. The private opening on Saturday night was by invitation only; the show would open to the public the following day. In spite of his outward casualness Edward had revealed far more of himself to her than she suspected he usually did, and it would be almost like a rejection of all that if she calmly ignored his moment of triumph.

On Friday Quinn phoned just as she was hurrying out the door to offer her a ride to Atlanta on Saturday morning. "No point in taking two cars," he reasoned. Grace told him she had planned to take a bus rather than risk getting herself lost in Atlanta traffic. She was proud of her cool, unemotional response until she realized she was systematically shredding the leaves of a curly Boston fern.

"Now that would be downright foolish, honey. I'm going to the same place you are, so we may as well double up and save energy. Besides, I haven't had time to ask how your battered shin is. You managed to get away before I could even speak to you the other night."

"You were busy."

"And you were suddenly in a terrific hurry," he drawled. Even on the phone his voice could affect her, raising the sensitivity of her nerve endings by several degrees!

"I'll pick you up about nine, then. We'll stay over and come back early Sunday afternoon, all right?"

"Whoa, there," she protested. "I hadn't thought about staying over."

With all the patience he must have developed over the years of looking after a large family, he said, "Grace, where's your common sense? These affairs go on till all hours, and if I know Edward, the champagne will flow pretty freely. I don't intend to risk having my insurance rates skyrocketed by picking up a DUI—not to mention the fact that I rather value both our necks."

"Which is precisely why I opted for the bus," Grace said tartly. "I can sleep all the way home."

"Honey, you may as well be sensible. I haven't the slightest intention of allowing you to dash all over Atlanta by yourself in the middle of the night. Besides, we'll have all the time in the world to talk on the long drive, and there are a few important things we have to clear up between us."

With that enticing proposition dangling before her, she was lost. Face it—she was addicted to the man. Until she was strong enough to kick the habit altogether, she couldn't resist the chance to spend practically a whole weekend with him.

If she had had trouble concentrating on her classwork before, she now found it impossible. All through the morning, when she should have been drilling her students in how to counteract all the various systems prompts, she was fighting off subliminal glimpses of herself and Quinn in an assortment of intimate situations. Her sigh of relief at the class-break buzzer was plainly audible, but she waited until the room was clear to go lean her forehead on the cool surface of the window.

There was a blue truck pulling into the parking lot on the other side of the new dorm site. A QD truck. Another sigh gusted out into the empty classroom as Grace watched Quinn swing out of the cab with the lithe gracefulness that was so characteristic of him—and so oddly unexpected in a man his size.

Five minutes. There was time enough to run out and say hello, to ask what time he wanted to leave. He had said nine, or thereabouts, but she could pretend to have forgotten.

Behave yourself, Grace Spencer! You're acting like an adolescent with her first crush!

She could at least step outside and wave—that would only be friendly. But even as she watched, a girl in pink overalls cut across campus to waylay Quinn as he strode onto the building site. Carly Johns, her brash red hair bouncing, had dashed up to stand panting before him, and while Grace watched, the girl talked and Quinn listened intently. His lips moved once, his distinctive brows lifted momentarily and then he placed one of his large, shapely hands on each side of Carly's face and kissed her on the forehead!

Oh, good Lord, woman, what does it take to get the message through your stupid skull? Quinn could no more resist a woman—*any* woman—than a bee could resist nectar! Even poor little besotted schoolgirls were fair game, and a grown man who would play fast and loose with an impressionable teenager was beneath contempt! Carly was no match for Donovan—*no* woman was a match for that chunk of molasses-coated machismo!

Grace wheeled away from the window, thoroughly disgusted and trying desperately to hide the truth from herself: she wanted to feel the touch of those large, work-honed hands on her own face.

She entered the corridor with no destination in mind just as Quinn came in the east door. He called out to her, but she had caught a glimpse of Elliot hurrying along to the drink machine and she dashed off after him. The machine was in a shallow alcove, clearly visible to anyone in the corridor, and Grace brushed off a fleeting twinge of conscience as she caught up with Elliot and curled a hand around his arm.

"Elliot! I haven't seen you around much lately," she greeted him, forcing an enthusiasm she was far from feeling.

She gave swift, silent credit to Mrs. Rand for her son's good manners. Startled, he smiled and patted her hand in a comically paternal gesture. "Not since the party, but I've been meaning to speak to you about something that's bothered me. Your sister . . ." His voice trailed off, and then, gathering determination, he plowed ahead. "I certainly hope I didn't foster any false impressions that day I showed her around the school. We stopped off for coffee on the way home, you know, and . . . well, the way she smiled at me . . . I mean, she's a lovely girl, in a . . . well, in a frivolous sort of way, and I was afraid she might have misunderstood my interest for something it wasn't. A man in my position—of course, Celia is a different sort—" He broke off with a look of embarrassed dignity, and Grace struggled to restrain the laughter that threatened her. Of all the pompous, overstuffed masculine egos!

When her amusement threatened to get out of hand, she impulsively reached up and kissed Elliot's soft, slightly pink cheek. Let him try explaining *that* to Celia!

Grace turned away, her eyes unconsciously sweeping the crowded hallway. She was in time to see a towering, Stetson-topped head disappear through the east door. Quickly subduing a dismaying rush of regret, she applied herself to getting through the rest of the day.

By eight thirty Saturday morning she was ready. She had changed clothes three times, finally settling on one of her more severe outfits, the brown suit, with a tailored white cotton shirt. Her hair was screwed up into an uncompromising knot at the back of her head and her steps were militant as she crossed to the porch to fill the demand feeder with dry catfood. They hated it, but if they were starving before she got back, they'd eat it.

She had thought of a dozen reasons why she shouldn't go to Atlanta and followed them up with a dozen reasons why she should. With her new sense of resolution, she convinced herself that it was an opportunity not to be missed, a chance to prove her immunity both to Quinn and to herself. Hadn't she begun that campaign yesterday when she had ignored his preemptory summons?

She'd ride with him, chat with him about the house, the region, the weather—any impersonal subject he cared to bring up. On the way back they could discuss Edward and his exhibit. Oh, there were any number of subjects two civilized adults could discuss without once touching on the personal. And she'd prove to herself and to him that she could easily withstand his charisma now that she understood it for what it was—a sham. An act designed to bolster his mammoth ego. Once, a long time ago, a woman named Allie had gotten off the hook, and since then he was compelled to try to reel in every female in sight, including minnows like poor little Carly.

She closed the door and locked it behind her when she heard the wheels of the black, racy sports car crunch onto her shelled driveway. At least she wouldn't be jouncing around in the hard-sprung pickup truck.

Quinn met her halfway across the front porch, a preoccupied half-scowl on his face. He snapped out something that sounded vaguely like a greeting.

Oh great! Looks like a promising start to the weekend!

He hooked her bag with a single finger and led her down the shallow steps, and only then did she see the slender, shapely arm resting on the passenger window.

"Will you have enough room in the back?" Quinn's voice was laced with what sounded like impatience. "Maggie gets carsick. She didn't think you'd mind." Her own comfort was obviously the last thing on his mind, Grace decided, as exasperation took the place of disappointment. By dint of a few extraordinary contortions she managed to insert herself into the minute space available.

By the time they had been driving for two hours, it occurred to her that the invalid was bearing up remarkably well. If Maggie Phillers was inclined to be squeamish, she managed to conceal the weakness beautifully! The drone of conversation from the front seat, largely one-sided, had kept on until Grace found herself nodding. At first she had attempted to listen, even though she wasn't all that fascinated by the running commentary of who owned what and how much it was worth. Nor, if Quinn's responses were anything to go by, was he. She stared at the back of his well-shaped head until the impulse to grab a handful of that dark, silver-edged crop of curls almost overcame her, and then she concentrated her attention on the woman.

Margaret Phillers must be at least thirty. She might have looked younger were it not for the chilly, calculating expression in her pale green eyes. At least it was chilly when they were turned to Grace; Quinn basked in a gaze of another sort altogether. She was attractive enough—actually she was almost beautiful. Her hair was a uniform shade of auburn, thick, shoulder length and quite dramatic with her pale, rather sallow complexion and her unusually light-colored eyes. She was not the sort of woman Grace craved for a friend, however, nor the sort she'd care to ask a favor of.

She awoke with a start to hear Quinn ask if she'd like to refesh herself. They were at a service station somewhere in the heart of Georgia, and a thick, cold fog had followed them up from the coast. Quinn helped her out, holding her hand while she regained the use of her cramped limbs.

"Sorry about that, Grace. Not much room back there, I'm afraid." He seemed about to say more when Margaret hurried across to tuck her hand under his elbow and bury her face in his shoulder.

"Ooooh, I'm *freezing!* Darling, let's *go!*"

"Get inside, then. Grace, stretch your legs and I'll get us all some coffee to go. Want a bag of boiled peanuts to munch on?"

"I hope you're just kidding!" She threw him a horrified look before trotting off in the direction of the ladies' room. She had yet to sample the southern delicacy—just the idea put her stomach in a peculiar mood.

By the time they reached Atlanta, Grace was sick of the perennial featureless gloom and she wondered if one could develop claustrophobia in a matter of a few hours. The dense fog was punctuated only by the hazy gleam of slowly moving traffic and the eerie glow of premature streetlights as Quinn homed in on the hotel nearest the gallery.

Grace blinked as her eyes adjusted to the sudden brilliance of the lobby. It was an older hotel, but from the richly appointed interior and the pleasant, if somewhat subdued atmosphere, she suspected it wasn't a particularly inexpensive one. Her bank account was already skimming the surface of thin ice without this!

Margaret claimed to be starving, and Quinn looked queryingly at Grace.

"Not for me, thanks. I'm going to soak the kinks out of my bones and then nap awhile and then I'll find a bite of something. Maybe the fog will clear off later on. What time are we expected at the gallery?"

Quinn consulted his watch. No thin gold disc for him; his was a large, stainless steel diver's watch with a utilitarian band. "About eight, or thereabouts. Go on up; I'll have something light sent up to your room in half an hour. Soak, eat and *then* nap," he ordered her, with a partial return of his old benign bossiness. Funny how she always seemed to end up on the receiving end of a dominant male. First her father, and now Quinn. Don Franklin had been at the other extreme—mild to the point of self-effacing, and look where that had got her!

"Come *on,* darling," Margaret insisted. "She's certainly old enough to look after herself, and I want to go shopping before tonight. There's a fantastic jewelry store right here in the hotel, and you haven't bought me my valentine yet." The lettuce-colored eyes took on a sparkle that Grace chose to think of as avaricious as both women continued to gaze up at Quinn.

The strain of the long, tedious drive was beginning to show. Grace didn't miss the tightening of his sensuous lips, nor the deepening of the attractive grooves that bracketed those lips.

"I'll be back as soon as I see Grace to her room. Wait here if you want to." The steeliness beneath the soft drawl was unmistakable. Grace meekly refrained from protesting that the bellhop was waiting to show her up. It was also sufficent to cause Margaret to subside into a sulky pout.

A silver-domed tray was waiting when Grace emerged from the bathroom half an hour later. She had no idea who had brought it inside, nor did she care. She was ravenous. She slid between the silky sheets, arranged a backrest of pillows and applied herself to polishing off the last drop of the rich, homemade vegetable soup. It reminded her of the soup made by her mother's cook, an iron-corseted woman who swore like a drill sergeant and cooked like an angel.

It could have been hours, or days, or only minutes later when she was aroused from a kaleidoscopic dream by a soft rap on her door. "Grace? Are you awake? Let me in," Quinn commanded quietly.

It took several moments for her to come to her senses. The dream merged with the strange hotel room and the eerie, mist-softened neon light outside. "I'm awake . . . I think. Is it time to get ready to go?"

"Not yet. Open the door, Grace, I want to talk to you."

"We can talk later. I'm not dressed." An understatement. She had slithered into bed just as she had come from the bath, delighting in the sensation produced by the cool, slick sheets on her rosy, bath-heated flesh.

"Put on a robe."

"I didn't bring one. Go away, Quinn!"

"Look, I don't care if you drape yourself in the bedspread, just open the door!" The impatient note in his voice dispersed the last of her sleep-induced mellowness and she wriggled upright to scowl at the door in question.

"Quinn, shut up and go away before you get us thrown out of the hotel! I have no intention of opening that door, and you can just darned well wait until I'm good and ready to come downstairs!"

Silence. Then, in ominously reasonable tones, he said, "Grace, aren't you being just the least bit childish? Look, regardless of what you're thinking, I only want to talk. It's been a long drive, and I worked until all hours last night just so I could take a couple of days off. I'll only keep you a minute."

He sounded exhausted, impatient—anything but amorous—and Grace yanked the bedspread loose and swirled it about her like a king-sized sari. "All right, but just for a minute," she grumbled, opening the door.

He sauntered in and her conscience smote her. He did look exhausted. He strolled across the room and dropped into one of the pair of lounge chairs, extending his long legs out in front of him with a sigh. Evidently a shopping trip with his girlfriend-secretary wasn't among the more restful ways to spend an afternoon.

"Where's Margaret?" Grace tucked the cumbersome wrap more securely about her as she settled herself into the other chair. Nearby, the disheveled bed gleamed like a snowbank under the glow of the bedside lamp.

"Getting dressed, I imagine. Maggie takes these things pretty seriously."

"Did you find her a proper valentine?" she sniffed, and then could have bit her tongue. It was exactly the sort of snide remark a jealous woman would make!

"She seemed to think so."

"How nice." The words were forced through clenched teeth as Grace waited for him to get on with whatever was on his mind. If this was some obscure war of nerves, Quinn had outscored her without even trying!

He seemed maddeningly content just to relax in comfortable silence. The top buttons of his white corduroy shirt were opened, baring the powerful tanned column of his throat, and Grace pinned her eyes desperately to the intricate pattern of the brocaded bedspread. Her feet were tucked up into the chair beside her, her arms wrapped defensively about her body.

"Aren't you going to ask what I brought you?" he inquired with mild curiosity.

Her head came up, sleep-clouded eyes searching his face warily. "Why should you bring me anything?"

"Why shouldn't I?" he countered easily.

She shifted her position in the confining folds of the heavy fabric. "Look, Quinn, whatever it was you wanted to say to me, say it and get it over with. I'm here to attend your brother's exhibit, not to play word games with you." And whether or not he was aware of it, her composure, unreliable at the best of times, was being seriously threatened by the undiluted potency of his masculinity! Neither his admitted tiredness nor her own common sense seemed to be any deterrent.

Lifting his lean hips in the chair, he shifted his weight and dug into one of his pockets, coming up with a small, domed leather box. The look he leveled at her was totally inscrutable as he tossed it into her lap, and Grace, ignoring the box, stared back at him in dismay.

"Aren't you going to look?" he asked after the second hand on his watch had made a full sweep.

Slowly she extracted an arm and a hand from the entanglement of the king-sized bedspread. She swallowed convulsively, acutely conscious of his enigmatic gaze on her as she flipped open the small box. A ring?

It was a pendant. Suspended from a flat, supple chain was a small gold cage encircling a heart fashioned of some strange, dark stone. She lifted it, entranced by the exquisite design, the intricate whorls of the cage as well as the unusual opaque stone. On closer inspection she could see that the deep blue surface of the small heart gleamed with tiny flecks of gold. "What is it?" she wondered softly, turning it in her hand.

"Lapis lazuli. Your stone. Didn't I tell you once that your eyes were the color of lapis?"

"I meant to look it up," she murmured, not taking her eyes from the delicate necklace. And then, feeling the intensity of his stare on her bared shoulders, her bent head, she did look up—right into the trap of his smiling eyes. Shaking herself free of his seductive sorcery, she said, "Quinn, I can't accept this. I mean, it's lovely—it's the most exquisite thing I've ever seen, but you know I can't—"

Like quicksilver, his mood reversed again. He stirred and then abruptly got to his feet, towering over her with poorly concealed impatience. "Don't be ridiculous. It's yours—no strings attached. I don't happen to know any other woman with gold-speckled navy blue eyes."

Reluctantly putting the expensive trinket back into its box, she said, "Any woman would adore it, no matter what color her eyes are. I've never seen anything like it before." She extended the box toward him, and he hunched his shoulders and wheeled away, refusing to look at her. "Keep it or throw it away—I couldn't care less! I'll buy you a box of fancy chocolates, then! Will your silly, hypocritical principles allow you to accept that?"

"There's nothing silly or hypocritical about my principles! Just because I—there's no reason to—why should you think . . . ?"

Oh, great Scott, she was incoherent again! Furious, embarrassed, absolutely *dripping* with love for the impossible wretch, and all she could do was babble about her stupid little principles!

She caught him just before he reached the door, stumbling on the enveloping folds of the bedspread. "Quinn, wait!" She tugged the spread up to cover what had nearly been exposed and yanked on his arm until he turned on her with a scathing look of impatience.

"I've waited a little too long as it is! I should have taken the bait the first time you threw it out, only it took me a while to discover who you were! Believe me, lady, if I'd bedded you before I learned the truth, there wouldn't be all this yammering about principles."

Grace sagged back as if he had struck her. The warm, gently teasing man she had once known had disappeared into this . . . this towering mountain of ice, and suddenly she wanted the old Quinn back. With all his exasperating teasing, his honey-coated charm, she had felt much safer than with this cold-eyed stranger.

Nothing he said made any sense to her. Neither his words nor the sudden changes in his moods. Where was the strong, sensitive man Edward had described to her, the gentle, teasing man she had come to love against all her better judgment?

Her eyes burned with a freshet of unwanted tears,

but before she could turn away to hide them, his hands closed over her shoulders with barely controlled force.

"I warned you, Grace. You picked the wrong man to play your little games with." And then, as if he were confused or had remembered something unsettling, he shook his head. "I keep forgetting," he muttered under his breath. His hands were still crushing the fragile bones of her shoulders.

"You forget what?" she managed to whisper.

"I forgot that it wasn't you who sent me all those love letters," he grated. His eyes burned accusingly into hers, as if compelling her to deny it, but it was all she could do to hang there, limply suspended from his powerful hands.

Bewildered, she searched his narrowed eyes for a clue. "I sent you *what?*"

His eyes slid away, but there was no disguising the heightened color in his lean, hollowed cheeks. Grace squirmed. "Quinn, I can't get a replacement for these shoulder bones, so if you don't mind?"

With a soft oath, he released her. Then, with lightning speed, his hands slid around her back, pulling her unceremoniously against him, which was infinitely worse! "There's no *time* now," he swore softly. "There's never any *time!* Any minute Margaret will show up to see if we're ready to go, and there'll still be all this business between us to clear up!" Her face was crushed against his soft corduroy shirt and she could hardly breathe, but she wouldn't have traded places with anyone in the world. "Meanwhile, in the few minutes we've got, I'm sure as the devil not going to waste time talking!" Without waiting for the protest that was the furthest thing from her mind, he captured her mouth and the battle was lost. As far as Grace was concerned, the whole war had been conceded a long time ago.

The flashpoint was reached instantly. With barely sheathed ferocity Quinn devoured her lips, taking everything, seeking still more, and she gave freely, from the very heart of her soul. His hands were everywhere, moving over her back to curve beneath her hips, stroking her satiny flanks, lifting her to insinuate her even closer to his thrusting masculine strength. He found her breasts, crushing them softly with trembling restraint, and then he held her away just far enough so that he could gaze down at her from feverish, heavy-lidded eyes. "You're killing me," he rasped, snatching her back to him to bury his face in her hair. "How did you manage to get in under my guard?"

She had no idea what he meant, nor was there any chance to ask. His mouth came down on hers and she was lost again, clinging frantically to the only reality in the universe.

Not until she felt the sharp edge of his belt buckle digging into her midriff did she realize that somewhere along the way, the bedspread had drifted to the floor unnoticed. They were standing near the door, and Quinn suddenly swung her up in his arms and turned toward the bed. Then, with a groan of raw agony, he put her down again. "Hell, Grace, are you deliberately trying to drive me over the edge? Look at you!"

She did. He had stepped back, raking a trembling hand through his unruly hair, and Grace swayed as he removed the support of his powerful arms. She took one stricken look at her own nakedness, her small breasts with their dusky, unabashedly aroused nipples framing the soft, imperceptible swell of her abdomen, and closed her eyes.

"A word of advice, Grace," he grated, his hands recklessly shoving his shirttail back inside the flannels that hugged his lean loins. "You'd better lower the voltage for that pasty-faced boyfriend of yours, or one of these days you're going to blow out his circuits!"

Grace was beyond speech. His voice came at her in uneven waves, like music from a distant radio station, and she breathed deeply, willing herself a thousand miles away from the untenable present. Her eyes were still closed tightly when she heard the door open and then close again, and the soft snick of the lock released the tears that could no longer be held back.

Chapter Nine

No stranger to her own weaknesses after all these years, Grace allowed the bout of tears to die a natural death. Then, as it had in the past, her instinct for survival began to rise to the surface. She lay there, taking in deep, steadying gulps of air as she considered her next move. To get up and dress, to accompany Quinn and Margaret to the opening was unthinkable; on the other hand, what else could she do? Hide here in her room like a frightened rabbit? What end would that serve?

She could call a cab and go to the bus station and hope there would be a bus back home within the next few hours. She rolled over on her back and stared up at the ornate ceiling. Why not? Quinn would be too busy squiring Margaret to come after her, even if he were so inclined. Not even in her most self-confident moments —and this was hardly one of them—could she imagine anything more unlikely. He had invited her to come to Atlanta with him because he was basically a generous man. If he had forgotten to mention the fact that he had another date for the weekend, was that a crime? And he had made a pass at her, not for the first time; but then for a man like Quinn, making a pass at a woman was as natural as breathing—or as calling every female in range of his caressing drawl "honey" or "darlin'."

Grace dragged herself from the tangle of bedcovers, crossed to the bathroom and splashed cold water over her face. It did little to diminish the puffiness around her reddened eyes, but it went a long way toward clearing her head. *"Honey,"* she murmured in cloying tones as she examined her ruined image in the mirror. *"Darlin'!"* And then, in a withering tone of voice, "Cornpone Lothario!"

By the time she had dressed in the white pointelle knit and twisted her hair up into a looser, far more flattering version of her usual classroom hairstyle, she was in an almost unnaturally calm frame of mind. She had admitted to herself in all fairness that Quinn's freedom with casual endearments was more a reflection of his own larger-than-life personality than a cheap, flirtatious ploy. After all, he'd hardly be trying to seduce the old woman at the fish market, would he? Basically a warm, generous man, he allowed the warmth to overflow when he was in an expansive mood. With a painful little parody of a smile, she recalled that in the tenderest of their most intimate moments, he called her by her name alone.

As for the peculiar references to love letters, the unnatural clarity of her mind had even gotten to the bottom of that. Elliot had often wondered how she managed to escape the practical jokes of their mutual students. The truth was, she hadn't—only she had been too dense to realize it. There had been that day last fall when she had forgotten her briefcase. When she found it the following Monday beside the copying machine, the papers had been jumbled out of order.

That could explain what Carly had been trying to tell her that day they had both been subjected to a heavy dose of Quinn's potent charm. There had been something on her mind, something, Grace thought in retrospect, that was connected to Donovan.

Could it possibly explain why Carly had run out to meet him yesterday? Had she confessed to sending him copies of Grace's poems?

Curiously enough, Grace was beyond embarrassment. None of it—the silly prank, the misunderstandings—had anything to do with her. In her present objective mood she could stroll into the gallery, greet Edward, smile coolly at Quinn and Margaret, look over the exhibit and then make her way to the bus station and go home. The steel of her backbone had been tempered in a pretty hot fire all those years ago, and it could only have strengthened with time.

A few minutes later she put down the phone with a disgruntled sigh. The trouble was, the buses weren't operating. The fog had everything shut down—planes, buses, even most of the street traffic.

Poor Edward. This was supposed to be his grand opening. Grace wandered over to lean on the windowsill and gaze down at the street below. There was some traffic. Not a lot, but some—guided by the soft, regular glow of the streetlights, no doubt, and the intermittent red and green haze of the stoplights. At most a third of those invited might be able to make it, and Grace knew she couldn't add to his disappointment. She was here, she was dressed and by darn she'd get there, Quinn Donovan or no Quinn Donovan!

Her militant resolution was interupted by Margaret's voice calling softly through the door. "Grace? Are you ready yet? Quinn's in a rotten mood, so I wouldn't advise keeping him waiting."

Grace opened the door and turned away, back erect, dark eyes snapping with determination. "I'll just be a minute. Let me get my coat."

The other woman didn't wait for an invitation to enter. She was stunningly overdressed in dark green satin harem pants with a gold lamé halter and jacket. In her ears were enormous, barbaric cubes of gold, studded with small, dark green stones. Emeralds? Probably!

"Like them? An early valentine. Ask for earrings and you get double the pleasure," she quipped with an air of sleek contentment. Grace half expected her to start purring.

"Lovely. They match your outfit beautifully."

"That's what Quinn thought," Margaret retorted smugly.

He probably gets these trinkets for all his women wholesale, Grace thought rancorously as she slipped her arms into the bulky winter coat. Her eyes moved involuntarily to the small, domed box on her dresser, and Margaret, following her gaze, reached for it, flipping it open. "Oh, aren't you going to wear yours? I told Quinn it would be embarrassing not to have something for you, since you happened to be our guest this weekend. Don't tell me you don't like my taste in costume jewelry. I thought it was so cute!" The small laugh that rippled out into the tense atmosphere was in no way reflected in those curiously pale eyes.

With the unnatural calmness that had accompanied her every action for the past half hour or so, Grace lifted the fragile chain from its bed of white satin and manipulated the intricate safety catch. She reached around under the bulky weight of her coat and fastened it, feeling the coldness of the metal and stone steal the warmth from the intimate valley between her breasts. Without once glancing in the mirror, she gathered up her gloves and purse, checked to be certain her key was inside and led the way to the door.

Bite the bullet, darn you! Bite the bullet!

Strangely exhilarated by the three-block walk to the gallery, Grace allowed Quinn to remove her coat and hang it up. Instead of waiting, she wandered into the brightly lighted room. Edward extricated himself from the small group of well-dressed patrons and hurried to meet her. He kissed her on each cheek, holding her hands in his warm ones after he stepped back to sweep her with an admiring gaze.

"You're still covered in fog, like the bloom on a grape," he laughed. "Lovely, lovely! Come thaw out while I get you some champagne."

"It seems to me that every time I see you, you're plying me with something intoxicating." It was easy to enter into the party spirit, easy to ignore the two people who had come to stand just behind her. She allowed Edward to lead her over to a long table laden with wheels of cheese, mounds of grapes, baskets of assorted crackers and a stunning array of delectable looking hors d'oeuvres. His hand hovered over the colorful punch and then moved on to accept a glass of sparkling champagne from a white-coated bartender. "I'm several ahead of you, so drink up. I want you well lubricated before you start making the rounds of my work."

"Doesn't say much for your self-confidence, ol' buddy," a familiar baritone drawled from behind her. Grace stared intently at a silver platter containing a roll of something brown in a congealed coat of clear green. It occurred to her that she had missed dinner. Under the circumstances champagne was a poor choice for a first course. She took a large swallow of the wine and turned a blinding smile on Quinn, forcing herself not to react visibly to the splendid figure he made in a near black lounge suit with an elegant gray and brick-red tie. He had worn a light-colored trenchcoat when they had left the hotel.

"I'm sure Edward's self-confidence is impregnable," she said coolly—the first words she had spoken directly to Quinn since he had taken an arm of each woman in the hotel lobby and guided them out into the cotton-candy night. "It must run in the family."

"Gotcha, Quinn!" the artist crowed in amused triumph, and he took Grace's arm and led her along the closest wall, pointing to the first of a series of enormous, colorful abstracts. "These first three are my Innocent Conceit period. After that comes the Uneasy Awakening period, and then the rest are pure How-Did-I-Land-Myself-in-This-Mess. Oh . . ." He pointed to a tall, thin canvas done in wavering tones of tawny reds with small, round, white accents. "Except for that one. That one's Ripple and Alka-Seltzer, otherwise known as Desperate Remorse."

Grace laughed unaffectedly. "Sounds as if that famous Donovan self-confidence has a few holes in it."

"You might say," Edward agreed wryly. "But so far nobody's seen through my act, so don't tip 'em off, will you?" He was leading her across the room to a grouping of small silverpoint drawings when they were intercepted by a tall, heavyset man who had evidently been sampling the liquid refreshments rather freely.

"This is absolutely the biggest load of hogwash I've seen this side of a pig farm, Eddie baby."

Grace almost lost her grasp on the slender stem of her wineglass. Her mouth dropped open and she forgot to close it as she waited for Edward's reaction. Before she could spring to his defense herself, though, the young artist laughed and clapped the offender on the shoulder. "You'd be the expert on that subject, you ol' son of a gun. But before you go on with your flattering critique, let me introduce you to my special guest. Grace, this lecherous sot is my good friend Farnum Taylor, the fourth. As if the first three weren't enough, his folks had to go and commit the ultimate folly. Folly, meet Grace Spencer—artist, poet and all-around inspiration who braved the fog to be with me in my moment of stark terror."

Farnum, who, to Grace's amusement, actually answered to Folly, accompanied them on their tour of the show. "How'd you get a respectable gallery to come across with a spread like this for you? The last one of these kneepants shindigs I got conned into going to served stale animal crackers and watered-down soda pop, and that was for an artist who could actually paint a barn that looked like a barn."

Grinning, Edward shook his head in mock admiration. "Grace, I hope you're suitably impressed with the impeccable taste of my inebriated friend. His idea of artistic subtlety is a plaster Venus with a matching lampshade on her head."

Undaunted, Folly cheerfully denounced the conspiracy of a few pseudointellectual con men to apply the emperor's clothing phenomenon to the art world. As the three of them strolled about, pausing frequently when one of the guests broke in with a question for the artist, Grace's attention wandered. She caught sight of Quinn from time to time, and always with Maggie clinging like a barnacle to his side.

"Stunning," someone exclaimed, claiming Edward's attention while Grace and Folly moved on, "but what does it really mean?"

Surprisingly, as Grace forced herself to turn her attention to the man at her side instead of allowing it to wander to the dark, curly head that towered over most of the assembly, she discovered that Folly Taylor was neither as inebriated nor as uninformed as he pretended. "I guess Eddie has his brother to thank for the quality of the feedbag," he confided. As they passed the refreshment table he collected them both fresh drinks. "These places don't normally run to this particular vintage, not even for a bright boy like Ed."

The talk gradually shifted from art to other topics. Grace, grateful not to be left on her own while Edward held court and Quinn entertained Margaret, listened as the expansive young man told her about stunt flying in something called a Pit Special—a plane, she assumed.

Through a break in the crowd she caught sight of Quinn. He seemed to be growing more morose as the evening wore on, and more than once she felt the impact of his lacerating gaze as she laughed at some outrageous remark of Folly's. Margaret was never more than three feet away from him, which made it the more surprising when the tall, auburn-haired woman slipped quickly into the lady's lounge behind her.

The door closed quietly and Margaret heaved an overdone sigh. "Lord, if I'd known the floors of this palce were marble, I'd have worn my track shoes!" She flopped on a pink leatherette sofa and examined a tortured foot in a transparent plastic mule with a four-inch gold heel. Then, looking up with a smile that merely rearranged the shape of her frosted, plum-colored lips, she said, "Is Folly giving you a lift home tonight?"

Grace's hands stilled in their task of re-achoring her chignon. Her eyes moved over the reflected image in the mirror, grudgingly acknowledging the stunning effect of the green and gold outfit on the green-eyed woman. The jacket had been shed, uncovering a halter that left little to the imagination. "Not that I know of. I think everything's socked in by the fog."

"Not Folly," Margaret snorted. She lighted a cigarette and drew deeply on it, sending a stream of blue smoke in Grace's direction. "Don't you know who he is? Lord, honey, you'll have half the women in three states on your neck after tonight. He's *only* the heir to FT Jetco—you know, they paste together those little executive model airplanes and peddle them to their friends?"

"Sorry—I'm not too bright when it comes to who's who in the South." Grace shoved in a hairpin with a vicious twist and then leaned over to tighten the strap on her sling-backed sandal.

"Oh, sure—little Miss Butter-Won't-Melt, in person. Well, for your information, Folly has to be at Jekyll sometime tomorrow to pick up a six-passenger job from some plutocrat who's decided to trade it in on a larger model. He told me he planned to drive back tonight and get an early start, and I'm sure he'd love to have company on the long drive home."

"Yes, but the fog," Grace said doubtfully. "I don't think . . ."

"Folly could find his way through solid concrete," Margaret announced. "He's got a radar system where most of us have eyes. Believe me, I've flown with the man in far worse than this. Besides, you'd be on your own tomorrow."

Frowning, Grace twisted around on the vanity bench. "On my own?"

"Quinn and I usually sleep late when we manage to slip away for a weekend." She laughed and the sound rippled unpleasantly across Grace's nerves. "Well, we have to sleep sometime! Quinn worked like a horse just so we could have a couple of days off, but if you don't mind hanging around on your own—we usually have breakfast in our room."

Our room. *Our* room! The words rang in Grace's

head. She forced her voice into a semblance of careless-
ness and said, "Oh, don't worry about me! Folly
mentioned something about"—she searched her brain
frantically for something plausible—"about waiting
until the fog burns off and going gliding," she announced triumphantly. *As soon as I sprout wings, that
is.*

The way back to the main gallery led directly past the
bar, and Grace helped herself to a fresh drink as she
passed. Arranging a brilliant smile on her face, she
turned to locate Folly and proceeded to walk blindly
into Quinn. The wine sloshed over the rim of her glass,
and he removed it from her fingers and placed it on top
of a sculpture stand alongside a tangle of welded
bronze.

"You're overdoing it, Grace. Get yourself something
to eat."

The tone of his voice, the hard glint in his eyes, the
very curl of his wide, sensuous mouth, brought every
fighting instinct in her to the surface. "Yes, Mr. Donovan, whatever you say, Mr. Donovan. Go to the devil,
Mr. Donovan." The words were sweetly spoken, and
then she turned and helped herself to another drink,
popped a grape into her mouth and wandered off, her
head at an uncomfortably high angle. At any moment
she expected to feel those steely talons biting into her
shoulders; instead she heard Margaret's plaintive voice
crying for help. "Oh, darn, Quinn, help me! My foot
skidded on these slick floors and I think I've hurt my
ankle! Oh, oh, my poor foot!"

As some of the starch drained out of Grace's spinal
cord, she drooped. "I can tell you what to do with your
poor foot," she muttered under her breath. "I can tell
you what I'd like to do with *mine!*"

"You were saying?" Folly questioned, coming up
behind her to drape a heavy arm across her shoulders.

"I was saying I'd give anything to be able to get back to Brunswick tonight instead of hanging around until Quinn feels like leaving tomorrow." There! She had committed herself; the next move was up to Folly.

Four hours later she was telling herself bitterly that she *ought* to be committed! The very idea of a mature, reasonably intelligent woman allowing herself to be pushed into such a lunatic action!

It had been ridiculously easy to talk Folly into slipping away and returning to the hotel with her to check out. She had barely had enough to pay her bill after refusing his generous offer to "take care of that little matter" for her. By the time he had stowed her bag in the back of an absurd open vehicle with a leather belt around its aristocratic snout—a Morgan, he had informed her loftily—second thoughts were rushing in a mile a minute. She was no longer certain he was sober enough to be trusted, but what else could she do? She had burned her bridges behind her with a vengeance. Even if she had the nerve to go back and tell the night clerk she had changed her mind about the room, she'd probably have to pay again, and she didn't have the money. The thought of having to wait and borrow it from Quinn, or even to explain to him what she was doing sleeping in the lobby, made up her mind for her. With a fatalistic sigh she told herself that at least he couldn't speed. The fog had lessened slightly, but visibility was still limited to fifteen or twenty feet or so.

"Do we have to go so fast?" she groaned for the third time as she clutched the damp leather seat with numb fingers.

"Honey, I've got clearance from the tower. It's now or never!" Folly Taylor drove the way he flew, she decided. Get up maximum speed in minimum time and hope for the best! They had left Atlanta behind, and now, on Interstate 75, they were meeting only the occasional glow of headlights. "We'll go to Tifton and then head east. Might run out of this stuff farther south," he yelled over the sound of the wind and the engine.

Grace was numb with a combination of cold and fear. Her stomach clamped down on the few morsels of solid food she had eaten at the party, and she regretted the several glasses of champagne. Folly's reflexes seemed unimpaired by the more than a few drinks he had had—although his judgment was up for questioning. As was her own!

By the time they passed Crisp, the fog was coming at them in patches, with intervals of drizzle. Folly, oblivious to the rain, was leaning forward, squinting into the darkness. "I'm going to cut across on 280 and then head southeast through Jessup. Hang on!"

She had no choice. Her fingers were frozen into a death grip on the hard leather upholstery. Somewhere behind her she thought there was a heap of canvas that might be a top. She opened her mouth to inquire about it and swallowed the words on a surge of nausea. Suddenly the cold, misty drizzle in her face was welcome.

Somehow the nightmare trip came to an end. The fog had returned as they neared the coast, and Brunswick was blotted out by a thick, peach-colored haze as the sun tried to break through. It had been a night out of time, an experience Grace could hardly believe she had undergone as Folly deposited her sodden bag on the doorstep. "You okay, baby?" he asked with belated solicitude.

"Who knows?" She was almost surprised not to find a white silk scarf and a goggled flying helmet surrounding the ruddy, grinning face.

"Gotcha here safe an' sound, huh? Rain or snow, hail or fog, ol' Folly always delivers. I'll give you a call when I get back in town, we'll take a spin over to Nassau, huh? Dad's got a little shack there. Say—you couldn't come up with a cuppa coffee for the road, could you? Those last few miles are killers!"

Closing her eyes on the urge to scream, she said, "Sure, if instant will do." After all, she had invited herself along on the drive—the least she could do was repay him with a cup of coffee. And the sooner he drank it and left, the sooner she could crawl into bed and die.

The house was thoroughly chilled. Grace went out to the kitchen in her coat and put the kettle on to boil. She opened the refrigerator and poured a bowl of milk for the cats. It seemed a thousand years since she had left them instead of just twenty-four hours. At least it wasn't as cold here as it had been in Atlanta. She had left the fire laid, and now she went back into the living room to strike a match to the wad of newspapers in the bottom of the stove. She found, to her consternation, that Folly had removed his leather topcoat and his shoes and was stretched out under her granny afghan on the yellow sofa, sound asleep.

"Oh, rats!" She wheeled away, leaving the fire unlighted, and switched off the kettle. Coffee could wait. There'd be no point in even trying to wake him now, not when he had consumed several glasses of champagne and then driven them halfway across the state. In the years of living on military bases Grace had known a few men like that—they reached a certain stage of inebriation where they could function with brilliant effectiveness, fooling all but the most astute. Ask them a question the next day, though, and they'd stare at you as if you'd wandered off a spaceship. Well, if poor Folly missed his appointment then that was just tough! He should have better sense than to drink and drive, especially in such horrible weather conditions.

And she ought to have her head examined for accompanying him, she jeered. She crawled wearily under the covers in her slip. Too tired even to change into her pajamas, she was asleep before her eyelids drifted down.

Sometime later she awakened by the sound of something falling, followed by a stream of highly original profanity. Squinting against the brilliant, clear light, she dragged herself out of bed and reached behind the door for her bathrobe, a utilitarian affair of white chenille. "I'm coming, I'm coming!" she yelled, wincing at the harsh sunlight pouring through her white organdy curtains.

"Where the blasted devil is the bathroom?" Folly cried pathetically. "You can't just hide a whole bathroom in a house this size."

"Oh, Folly, stop screeching. It's on the back porch!" She pointed the way, and after he had stumbled through, she lighted the fire and made her way out to the kitchen to plug in the kettle . . . again. Five minutes or so of moving about took the edge off her own discomfort, and she was actually whistling tunelessly under her breath when the wretched looking man lurched back into the room. His formerly ruddy face had taken on a distinctly greenish tinge.

"Coffee?"

"Coffee."

"Breakfast?"

He cast her a speaking look. "Just get some coffee in me and I'll see if I can make it out to Jekyll. I've got to fly that blooming thing back and then go on to Cincinnati before tonight."

Wordlessly she handed him a steaming mug of black coffee. How on earth could any man drive like a bat all night long and then be expected to fly all day? Especially when his brain was all but pickled in alcohol! "Have a piece of dry toast, at least. It can't kill you."

"Would you mind checking to see if the top of my head's still there?" he asked with exaggerated politeness, and Grace found herself massaging the back of his neck and his temples, with their visibly throbbing veins. She was still at it a few minutes later when the back door burst open and Quinn appeared, looking almost as wretched as poor Folly.

Of the three of them it was Folly who recovered the use of his tongue first. "Howdy, Quinn baby. Don't breathe so heavily, if you don't mind. Got a dyin' man here."

Without daring to look directly at him, Grace knew Quinn was in an explosive temper. The small kitchen fairly rocked under the barrage of silent anger. The fingers that had been momentarily paralyzed by his sudden appearance nervously resumed their ministrations. She kept her eyes focused on the top of Folly's dark blond hair—which, she noticed abstractedly, was growing distinctly thin on top.

"Would you mind telling me exactly what's going on here?" Quinn enunciated slowly. Each word was released as carefully as if it were riding on a bed of TNT.

"I'm getting my head put back together, and this little angel here—what was your name, honey?" the seated man asked plaintively.

Grace blinked in disbelief. He was joking. She had known he was in bad shape, but not that bad! Her fingers trailed away and she waited for what came next.

Nothing did. The man was patently waiting for her to tell him her name. He didn't remember a blessed thing about last night and their reckless, miserable trip from Atlanta! "Edward," she blurted, with an idea of reminding him where they had met.

With comical emphasis, he repeated, *"Ed*-ward! 'S a funny name for a nice li'l gal like you! Honey, do that place down on my back again, will you? Yeah—a little more of that an' I might even live!"

It would have been funny if it hadn't been so pathetic—and if Quinn hadn't been looming over them like an ancient, vengeful deity. The beginning of a smile faded from her face and she stepped back hastily before Quinn's thundering anger. Before she could protest his brutal behavior, he lifted the other man and frog-marched him toward the front door, collecting his shirt, coat and shoes as they went. He opened the door, ejected the foolishly grinning Folly and tossed his belongings after him.

Then he turned to Grace, who stood frozen in the kitchen door. "I'll give you two minutes to tell me just what in blazes is going on, and woman, it had better be good," he said with a chilling lack of emphasis.

Chapter Ten

Grace's first impulse was to run into her bedroom and slam the door. It took only one glance at the implacable set of Quinn's jaw to assure her that escape was out of the question. She might as well try to hide from a tidal wave.

"Would you care for a cup of coffee?" she ventured placatingly. Then, as her face slowly lifted to the height required for eye contact, her weathervane mood swung around again. Anger at his high-handed interference in her affairs rose to choke her, and her delicately arched brows came down in a level scowl. Why should she feel obligated to placate Donovan? "Look, why don't you just butt out of my life? I don't *need* you charging in here and throwing people around! I don't need *any* man snapping out orders and expecting me to obey!"

"Get some clothes on," Quinn ordered grimly, as if she hadn't even spoken. There was a hollow-eyed look to him that struck her unexpectedly, lowering her anger from boiling point to a slow simmer.

Grace stared in growing frustration at the broad shoulders. They were slightly hunched now, and if she hadn't known better she would have described his stance as defensive. He still wore the suit he had worn last night—or at least, part of it. The dark trousers minimized his lean, taut hips, skimmed the muscular strength of his powerful thighs, and the once pristine white shirt had been wrenched open at the throat, the cuffs turned back over heavily muscled, darkly haired forearms. Even exhausted, Quinn carried with him a force that couldn't be ignored—a masculine vitality that burned from his tired eyes like glowing coals.

Taking the coward's way out, Grace backed slowly, quietly into her bedroom, snatched up a handful of clothes without even bothering to look at them and scurried into the bathroom. With any luck at all, he'd be gone by the time she emerged.

She bathed and dressed herself in yellow jeans and her purple shirt—not a combination she would have selected deliberately, had she been aware of it. Her mind had gradually begun to function again, if not at peak efficiency. Reluctantly she admitted to herself that she owed Quinn an apology for running out on him after he had given her a ride and booked her into the hotel. With his exaggerated sense of responsibility, he had probably worried when she had turned up missing.

When she could no longer rationalize hiding in the bathroom, she emerged, half hoping Quinn would have lost patience and left by now. He was standing in the doorway between the two main rooms, staring at the spool-legged table filled to overflowing with potted plants, as if the speckled leaves of the begonia held the secret of cosmic order.

"Uh—Quinn, I think I should apologize. I mean, I

do—apologize, that is," she stammered. He looked wretched, as if he hadn't been to bed in a week.

The unexpected flow of an almost maternal warmth fled as soon as he turned to face her. All the old arrogance was back—in the angle of his head, in the very way he carried himself. No five-star general she had ever met carried himself with more of an air of command!

Suddenly Grace felt more threatened than ever. "Forget it!" she snapped, crossing her arms belligerently. No matter how badly she had behaved, he had no right to burst in here and look at her as if she were less than the dust beneath his king-sized boots!

"Did you spend the night here with him, or did you stay over at his apartment in Atlanta and leave this morning?"

"I don't consider that any of your business!"

With two great strides he was standing in front of her, and all reason deserted her. Her instinctively defensive anger scattered to the four winds, leaving her with only a quaking sort of hollowness. To her over-stimulated imagination he seemed to have grown larger, more threatening than ever.

"I—w-we—" Before she could do more than chatter a few stumbling words, he clamped his hands on her arms and lifted her until only her toes touched the floor. "Quinn, please! You're hurting me!"

He shook her then. "I ought to put you over my knee and peel the hide off you! Do you have any idea—do you have the *slightest* conception of what I went through when you disappeared last night with that irresponsible, womanizing flea-brain?" He shook her again, his enormous strength barely under control, but when she winced at the pressure of his iron-sinewed fingers, he allowed his grip to ease to a bearable level.

Sheer bravado kept her from dropping her glaring

eyes from his. "Womanizing! That's great, coming from you!"

Something almost like pain darkened his eyes momentarily, and she muttered grudgingly, "All right, I suppose I could have told you."

"Told me! *Told* me!" He blazed down at her, and she wondered why she had ever considered him warm, genial, even tenderhearted. He was a raging cyclone!

"Do you know what I thought? Have you any idea of what went through my mind when Maggie told me you and that—that lush had left together? When I discovered that you'd checked out of the hotel?" His voice was a raw parody of his old drawl. "You were either flying with him, driving with him or sleeping with him, and for the life of me, I don't know which would have been worse!"

"We were driving, Quinn," she whispered, helpless before the feelings he aroused in her, even in his anger.

Illogically he lit onto her words. "He drove back in that fog? With *you* along with him? God!" His eyes closed momentarily, then opened to move over her in an anguished sweep, taking in her pallor, the trembling of her mouth. "Don't you ever—*ever*—put me in that position again. You are not, I repeat, *not* to get in a car, a plane, a boat or even a blasted tricycle with anyone who's been drinking! Is that clear?"

When she didn't answer—couldn't answer for the fury that was once more rising inside her—he added, "Woman, you need a keeper!"

It was the wrong thing to say. It was entirely too reminiscent of her father's arbitrary ordering of her early life. She took a deep, steadying breath and then began to speak—grimly, flatly. "All right, Quinn, you've had your say, and maybe you're entitled to it. But let's get something straight—I don't answer to you. I don't answer to any man, not ever again. If you were worried, then I'm sorry. I—it seemed like the thing to do at the time." She paused then, uncertainty beginning to seep in as he continued to stare at her in a way she found increasingly disconcerting. "I mean, under the circumstances—well, when Maggie said—"

"*Maggie* said! What does Maggie have to do with anything?"

Bitterly she replied, "A lot, I should think. Anyway, it suited me just fine to come back early. If the buses had been running, I wouldn't have considered riding with Folly, but honestly, I didn't know he was in such bad shape. I thought a bit of cold air—Maggie said—"

Enough of Maggie said! Maggie was a painful subject between them. "Look, Quinn, if you were worried about me, I'm sorry. But I'm fine now. I'm just fine!"

What was the use? He felt responsible for her only because he had driven her to Atlanta, escorted her to the opening, and she didn't want his concern—not *that* way. He was a caring man, Edward had said. Landed with the responsibility of a large family at an early age, he had developed the habit of looking after anyone and everyone weaker than he—a criterion that would include ninety-nine percent of the people he met.

Well, she was not one of his strays. She didn't *need* looking after! Stroking the defensive fires of her anger, she told herself that if that was the only reason he was here, then the sooner he left, the sooner she could start getting him out of her system!

"All right, I apologize! I was rude, ungrateful, discourteous and anything else you care to heap on my plate! I ruined your weekend for you by barging in where I wasn't wanted in the first place, and then, when I tried to back out and leave you two some time together, I only made matters worse! So sue me! Write an irate letter to the editor, only get out of my house now, and leave me alone! I don't *need* you, Quinn

Donovan! I can manage my life without any big honcho telling me when to stand and when to sit down! I grew up with that sort of male domination and I'm not about to take any more of it!"

Into the thunderous silence that followed her outburst, the sound of the kitchen sink dripping into a coffee mug could be heard. Plink, plunk.

Everything about this blasted place needed fixing—maybe she'd better cut her losses and get out of here! She'd go to Saint Louis, or . . . or Santa Fe. Somewhere. *Any*where! She'd start over where there'd be no overbearing, aggravating, dominating man to undermine her hard-earned independence.

At first, when Quinn repeated her words out of context, she didn't recognize them. *"Our weekend? Just whose weekend did you think it was supposed to be, Grace?"*

It took several moments to pull her thoughts back from her determination to escape Quinn's meddling interference. She applied herself once more to clearing the slate between them, once and for all. "Yours. Yours and Margaret's, and there's no supposing about it!"

The burden of weariness that had settled itself onto Quinn's shoulders seemed to grow perceptibly heavier as he raised a hand to his forehead, massaging the furrows that had suddenly appeared there. Grace waited, mesmerized by the hint of vulnerability in the otherwise impregnable man. "Margaret," he sighed, and something in the resigned way he said the name brought a tight fist to close sickeningly around her stomach. The room seemed to recede until the only reality was the man before her—the darkly arched brows, the thick mustache, the dramatic hair and the tanned, rugged features.

"Quinn," she cast out a little desperately, "would

you care for some breakfast?" It suddenly occurred to her that she hadn't eaten more than a few grapes since the soup she had had in bed at the hotel the day before. No wonder she was feeling woozy!

"That might not be a bad idea," he conceded tiredly. "Let's go to my place. At least there I can be sure of more than a butterfly's portion."

On the verge of flying off the handle again, she sighed in unconscious submission. She had about three eggs in the refrigerator, and no bacon, and she was suddenly ravenous.

Church was letting out and traffic was stop-and-go until they left the town behind. The sound of the church bells echoed briefly, and then there was only the purr of all that horsepower under the hood of Quinn's car. Grace leaned her head back and closed her eyes until the sound of shell crunching beneath the tires alerted her to their whereabouts. It occurred to her that she was out of her mind to come meekly along like this. She should have said her piece, let him read the riot act over her head and then sent him on his way. This was only prolonging the agony. Her only excuse was the raw need in her, a need that was bound to grow worse before it grew better.

"There's something you need to see while I cook us some breakfast. Maybe after eating, we can talk without the fireworks." He smiled at her tiredly.

Mollie trotted around the house to greet her, then returned to a spot of sunshine at the edge of the marsh. Grace said nothing as she followed Quinn to the door. Since she had last seen the place, the windows had been installed in the main house, and it struck her that it was really an enormous place for a bachelor. But maybe he didn't intend to remain a bachelor. At the thought, her

177

heart leaped and then subsided into a cold, hard knot. The house had been planned and started long before he had ever laid eyes on Grace Spencer. If he had any plans to increase the size of his immediate family, they didn't include her.

"Omelets suit you?" he asked, crossing to one of the built-in cabinets that formed the storage wall. He removed a sheaf of papers that Grace recognized immediately as being photocopies.

"Maybe you'd better see these," he murmured, placing them in her hand and disappearing into the compact kitchen.

Before she even lowered her eyes to the crisp copy, she knew what it would be. *"Rose pink are your lips, my love, Iris blue, your eyes. Forget-me-not, for in your hands, My happiness yet lies."* The words, written in her distinctive handwriting and initialed with the small, ambiguous GBS, were flawless photocopies. "From your Secret Admirer"—was written in blue ink. Oh, Lord!

She set it aside and read another. It struck her ears with an almost saccharine sweetness, seen out of the context of the valentine format. The signature, this time, was a skillful copy of her own first name. "Yours lovingly, Grace."

With numbed fingers she reached for yet another one and read the familiar lines. *"Daisies have a secret; Roses have one, too. Listen with your heart, my dear, They'll tell you I love you."*

Dropping the paper onto the small pile, she closed her eyes against the painful emotions that wracked her small frame. All the secret glances, the quickly hushed giggles among the girls, came back to her. Now that she was aware of what had happened, so many things made sense—remarks that had been greeted with gales of laughter, but that had left her with that baffled feeling of helplessness, as if all the world knew a secret at her expense.

Which was little less than the truth, she thought, feeling suddenly depleted. As a teacher, she was not a rousing success. She had reacted badly to the first setback, and from then on she'd been afraid to lighten up, afraid of losing the little control she had over them. And they had been quick to sense her fear.

With a low, anguished groan her thoughts turned in another direction. No wonder Quinn had thought she was giving him the come-on! If he had read all these florid, fervid missives, he must have thought she was desperate for any man's attention! And then, when she had rebuffed his perfectly understandable advances, he must have taken her for a tease—or worse!

He emerged from the kitchen to place the heaped plates on the table, and Grace averted her face. How he must have laughed at her! He must have known almost from the first who had written this—this *drivel!* Despite the fact that no last name had been given, Grace wasn't all that common a name among women her age.

"Ready to eat?" His voice held a note of tenderness that made her want to curl up and die. He held a chair, and she dragged herself up reluctantly from the womb-like security of the deep cushions.

"When did you get them?" she asked with grim resolution. The embarrassing topic wasn't going to disappear by ignoring it.

"Salt and pepper? The first one came a day or so before I ran into you out beside the marsh."

"You do know that I had nothing to do with it, don't you?" she muttered as she slathered butter furiously across the surface of her toast.

"Sure. I'll admit, I wondered at first, but after a while it occurred to me that the real author wouldn't have mailed me photocopies—unless she had a heart like a boomerang." His grin was almost up to his old standards.

"Hmmm." She frowned, taking a large bite of the succulent omelet. Another KSO special, this time with bits of chicken liver and mushrooms in a cheese and tomato sauce. "How'd you find out?"

"You mean who wrote them or who mailed them?"

"Both." She refused to look at him. It was enough to feel the vibrations radiating from his powerful body, stunning even now, when he was exhausted, rumpled and had more than a shadow of beard on his aggressive jaw.

"When Ogleby forwarded your letter about the sunken bathroom—"

"And kitchen."

He went on as if she hadn't interrupted. "I recognized the handwriting. You make your G's in a unique way. Back when the first one came, I was amused. That was the secret admirer version. When they kept on coming, one or two a week, I was intrigued, and I was determined to find out who sent them. By the time I got the note from Ogleby, I had—well, you might say, run into you a few times, and I was more intrigued than ever. In the first place you hardly seemed the type. All hedgehog prickles—you certainly didn't seem to think much of me at close range. Even so, I couldn't figure out why you seemed to blow hot and then cold."

"Oh, Lord," Grace mumbled, hiding her face behind the utilitarian-sized coffee cup.

"Yeah—well. I rushed my fences, you balked, I backed up and tried again, and for the life of me, I didn't know whether I was coming or going." He pushed away his plate and tipped his chair back at a perilous angle. "The thing was, I'd erected this

. . . well, you might say, a barricade, over the years. Oh, I like women as well as the next man."

He grinned that overwhelming, undermining grin of his, and Grace felt her defense systems shutting down, one after another. "But, you see, something happened once when I was still pretty damp behind the ears. I stuck out my thick neck and had it chopped off by a little gal I sort of fancied at the time. Figured after that I'd be better off playing by a certain set of rules."

Desperately Grace tried to marshall all the reasons why she couldn't afford to succumb to his spell. *Watch it, girl—he's warning you off in his nice, molasses-coated style!*

"Only you didn't play by my rules. You didn't play by anybody's rules! I'm a sweet, considerate, reasonable sort of guy—the type who can handle most anything that comes along without too much trouble, by applying certain logical principles. Only I hadn't figured on anything like you." He took her arm and urged her unresisting body away from the table, to the Indian rug-covered daybed. At the last minute she panicked, twisting away and dropping into a deep, suede-covered armchair instead. She had problems enough dealing with this creature without her libido's getting involved!

"What are all these logical principles you keep spouting about?" she temporized. Keep it impersonal; principles are one thing, personalities another!

"Honey, at this point I'm concerned with just one thing, and it sure as the devil isn't logic. But I'll tell you this much—I've always known what I wanted, even if I haven't always recognized it when it came along. And I want you. And before you open that stubborn little mouth of yours and start spouting off a lot of nonsense, I'd better make something else clear to you."

The stubborn little mouth was open, all right—

hanging from its hinges, only no sound was issuing forth. Grace wasn't at all sure she could trust her ears, and she certainly knew better than to trust her tongue. It had a way of betraying her at awkward moments.

"I've told you about my family. They're all scattered around now, busy with their own affairs, but that doesn't mean they aren't my family. I'm building a home large enough so that if any of them ever need a bolt hole, they'll have it. I want 'em to feel free to get together here on Christmas and Thanksgiving. I want to know all my nieces and nephews, and my lady will have to accept the fact that just because I love her to the ends of the earth and then some, that doesn't mean I love them any the less."

Grace couldn't have spoken then if her life depended on it. She was seeing Quinn's outsized form against the light from the sliding glass doors, and it cast a shimmering halo around him. She wasn't even aware of the tears that trembled on her lashes, magnifying the radiant effects of the light.

"So you see, Grace, it has to be a whole-hearted commitment. It takes a tremendous person to put up with me and all my old-fashioned nonsense, but I can't change. I can only ask you to make the effort—if you care for me enough."

Somehow she managed to get the words past the lump in her throat. "If I *care* enough! Oh, Quinn, don't you honestly know?"

"Honey, if I did I wouldn't have gone through what I went through last night." Grace caught a glimpse of the agony he referred to before the control came down over his melting dark eyes, and it staggered her. "I dumped poor old Maggie out on her front stoop and came charging out to your place breathing fire!"

Ruefully, but with a warmth she didn't even try to

hide, she teased him. "You were doing that, all right. I was about to send for Saint George." Her eyes were clinging to him like moss on the north side of a tree.

"Honey, you don't need to send for anyone. You can handle any dragon I've ever met all by yourself."

"Well—maybe, at least if he's only a cornpone dragon, like you."

He reached for her then, pulling her out of the chair and onto the daybed beside him, and it was all she could do not to wrap her arms around his waist and bury her head in the strength and security of his arms. Not yet, though—a vestige of wariness held her back from committing herself fully. "About Margaret," she began with a convincing show of coolness.

"Margaret," he sighed. "My whole weekend began to go sour when Margaret invited herself along. I couldn't figure out how to get rid of her without hurting her feelings. Poor old Maggie doesn't have much luck when it comes to finding herself a man, and as aggravating as she can be, a fellow can't help feeling sorry for her."

Grace made a mental note to help poor old Maggie find a man of her own—perferably several hundred miles away.

"And then you rejected the special valentine I had made for you. I had counted on that, you know. I figured a woman with as much romance in her heart as you have would appreciate a little trinket like that, and I had a goldsmith in Savannah make it up for me."

Her lapis heart! Her own special valentine that was even now tucked away in her purse.

He laughed in half-rueful embarrassment. "I was going to come up with some sort of flowery speech and hope you wouldn't laugh me out of town, but somehow nothing worked out the way I'd planned it. There were

183

all these other fellows hanging around you—I saw red, and believe me, sweetheart, it wasn't valentines! I'd felt like taking your old boyfriend, Rand, apart that day when I saw you kiss him."

She had to break in then. "I was jealous. I'd seen you kiss Carly just before that, and it—"

"Carly Johns? Grace, the poor tad was in tears, confessing to what I'd already just about figured out. You see, precious, I knew who wrote the love poems, but I couldn't be quite certain who'd mailed them to me. To tell you the truth, I didn't want to know. I wanted it to be you, and I was afraid it hadn't been. When that poor little redhead owned up, I kissed her to keep from spanking her, although I don't think she was the real ringleader."

His hands were tracing patterns on the sides of her neck, and when they slipped under her shirt to seek out the small hollows of her shoulder, Grace tried to control her crazy impulses. Then Quinn pulled her over to lie on top of him, and she could feel every thundering beat of his heart. Before she surrendered the last bit of her prickly, tender pride, however, there were one or two things that had to be cleared away, because once the talking stopped, she suspected it would be a long time before it resumed again.

"Quinn, are you sure there's nothing between you and Maggie? I mean, after all, a man doesn't normally give his secretary emeralds unless she's outstandingly good at—at shorthand."

"Emeralds! You mean those green glass things she picked out? Well, as a matter of fact, I felt a little embarrassed because I had had the heart made for you—I was planning on its being an engagement present. I had ordered a bushel or so of red roses and daisies to be delivered to your room with your breakfast this morning—sort of a subtle hint, you might say. Then, when Maggie invited herself along, I felt guilty as the devil because I resented her so much. If she'd offered to take herself off somewhere, I'd have bought her the store." He grinned, slowly releasing the last button on her blouse from its buttonhole. "I'm afraid I'm not too good when it comes to romance. I'm better at accomplishing things with my hands—which is why I still like to climb aboard the dozer now and then and make things happen." His eyes were endearingly apologetic, and Grace decided that one of these days she'd let him know just how skilled he was at making things happen with those hands of his.

The last of her doubts drifted into nothingness, like the morning fog under a rising Georgia sun. "Oh, Quinn, when it comes to being a romantic, you win, hands down. But when it comes to loving, you've met your match. As big as you are, I'm not sure you're big enough to handle all the love I have for you."

The gauntlet was down. He picked it up. "Woman, I never refuse a dare. Starting now, you're going to prove your words. That ought to take a couple of decades, at least, and then we'll need a few more for me to prove mine, so we'd better not wait around too long to get started. There's no waiting before or after a marriage license in the state of Georgia, you know."

His hands were making slow, soothing movements on her body that were anything but soothing! She tugged the shirt that she'd already unbuttoned out from his pants and raked her fingernails down the powerful muscles of his back, delighting in his immediate response. "Say it, Quinn—you haven't told me yet." With every look, every touch of his hands, he was telling her, but she needed to hear the words.

"Can't you hear me, Grace? I'm saying it—I've been saying the words to you for so long now."

And when her beseeching eyes moved past his aggressive chin, past the stern, yet tender mouth, the sensuous brush of his mustache and the proud thrust of his nose, to the melting warmth of his dark eyes, he whispered, "Listen with your heart, beloved."

Silhouette ❦ *Romance*

15-Day Free Trial Offer
6 Silhouette Romances

6 Silhouette Romances, free for 15 days! We'll send you 6 new Silhouette Romances to keep for 15 days, absolutely free! If you decide not to keep them, send them back to us. You pay nothing.

Free Home Delivery. But if you enjoy them as much as we think you will, keep them by paying the invoice enclosed with your free trial shipment. We'll pay all shipping and handling charges. You get the convenience of Home Delivery and we pay the postage and handling charge each month

Don't miss a copy. The Silhouette Book Club is the way to make sure you'll be able to receive every new romance we publish before they're sold out. There is no minimum number of books to buy and you can cancel at any time

This offer expires July 31, 1983

Silhouette Book Club, Dept. SBX 17B
120 Brighton Road, Clifton, NJ 07012

Please send me 6 Silhouette Romances to keep for 15 days, absolutely free. I understand I am not obligated to join the Silhouette Book Club unless I decide to keep them.

NAME_____

ADDRESS_____

CITY_____STATE_____ZIP_____

Silhouette Romance

IT'S YOUR OWN SPECIAL TIME

Contemporary romances for today's women.
Each month, six very special love stories will be yours
from SILHOUETTE. Look for them wherever books are sold
or order now from the coupon below.

$1.50 each

Hampson	☐ 1. ☐ 4 ☐ 16 ☐ 27 ☐ 28 ☐ 52 ☐ 94	Browning	☐ 12 ☐ 38 ☐ 53 ☐ 73 ☐ 93
Stanford	☐ 6 ☐ 25 ☐ 35 ☐ 46 ☐ 58 ☐ 88	Michaels	☐ 15 ☐ 32 ☐ 61 ☐ 87
		John	☐ 17 ☐ 34 ☐ 57 ☐ 85
Hastings	☐ 13 ☐ 26	Beckman	☐ 8 ☐ 37 ☐ 54 ☐ 96
Vitek	☐ 33 ☐ 47 ☐ 84	Wisdom	☐ 49 ☐ 95
Wildman	☐ 29 ☐ 48	Halston	☐ 62 ☐ 83

☐ 5 Goforth	☐ 22 Stephens	☐ 50 Scott	☐ 81 Roberts
☐ 7 Lewis	☐ 23 Edwards	☐ 55 Ladame	☐ 82 Dailey
☐ 9 Wilson	☐ 24 Healy	☐ 56 Trent	☐ 86 Adams
☐ 10 Caine	☐ 30 Dixon	☐ 59 Vernon	☐ 89 James
☐ 11 Vernon	☐ 31 Halldorson	☐ 60 Hill	☐ 90 Major
☐ 14 Oliver	☐ 36 McKay	☐ 63 Brent	☐ 92 McKay
☐ 19 Thornton	☐ 39 Sinclair	☐ 71 Ripy	☐ 97 Clay
☐ 20 Fulford	☐ 43 Robb	☐ 76 Hardy	☐ 98 St. George
☐ 21 Richards	☐ 45 Carroll	☐ 78 Oliver	☐ 99 Camp

$1.75 each

Stanford	☐ 100 ☐ 112 ☐ 131	Browning	☐ 113 ☐ 142 ☐ 164 ☐ 172 ☐ 191
Hardy	☐ 101 ☐ 130 ☐ 184	Michaels	☐ 114 ☐ 146
Cork	☐ 103 ☐ 148 ☐ 188	Beckman	☐ 124 ☐ 154 ☐ 179
Vitek	☐ 104 ☐ 139 ☐ 157 ☐ 176	Roberts	☐ 127 ☐ 143 ☐ 163 ☐ 180
Dailey	☐ 106 ☐ 118 ☐ 153 ☐ 177 ☐ 195	Trent	☐ 110 ☐ 161 ☐ 193
		Wisdom	☐ 132 ☐ 166
Bright	☐ 107 ☐ 125	Hunter	☐ 137 ☐ 167
Hampson	☐ 108 ☐ 119 ☐ 128 ☐ 136 ☐ 147 ☐ 151 ☐ 155 ☐ 160. ☐ 178 ☐ 185 ☐ 190	Scott	☐ 117 ☐ 169 ☐ 187
		Sinclair	☐ 123 ☐ 174
		John	☐ 115 ☐ 192

$1.75 each

Silhouette Romance

Coming next month from
Silhouette Romances

Sunset in Paradise by Carole Halston

When Aunt Liz sold their house to the wealthy and handsome Jonathan Talbot, Fran's carefree days in Key West seemed numbered . . . until she made herself part of the deal.

Trail Of The Unicorn by Cathryn LaDame

Working for her uncle at the Unicorn Society Institute was very different from working under arrogant Thane Fraser out in the field, where Lesley knew she'd have to fight to prove her ability.

Flight Of Fancy by Laura Eden

Lisa Ashton wanted only two things in life and neither included the devastatingly handsome Serge Devereaux . . . until he offered her the job she wanted with his aviation firm!

Greek Idyil by Jade Walters

Rosalie Darrien wanted to teach the wealthy Louis Alexander that a pretty girl was more than a mere toy to be played with—but in the process she fell under his spell.

Yesterday's Promise by Karen Young

Late hours at a Boston engineering firm left Julie Dunaway no time for love until the dynamic new consultant they hired turned out to be her estranged husband.

Separate Cabins by Janet Dailey

When Gardiner MacKinley met Rachel MacKinley aboard the Mexican Rivieria cruise, he wanted to share more than just a last name, but could Rachel believe his tender vows for the future?

READERS' COMMENTS ON SILHOUETTE ROMANCES:

"I would like to congratulate you on the most wonderful books I've had the pleasure of reading. They are a tremendous joy to those of us who have yet to meet the man of our dreams. From reading your books I quite truly believe that he will some-day appear before me like a prince!"

—L.L.*, Hollandale, MS

"Your books are great, wholesome fiction, always with an upbeat, happy ending. Thank you."

—M.D., Massena, NY

"My boyfriend always teases me about Silhouette Books. He asks me, how's my love life and natu-rally I say terrific, but I tell him that there is always room for a little more romance from Sil-houette."

—F.N., Ontario, Canada

"I would like to sincerely express my gratitude to you and your staff for bringing the pleasure of your publications to my attention. Your books are well written, mature and very contemporary."

—D.D., Staten Island, NY

*names available on request